CROSSING
JHORDAN'S RIVER

CROSSING
JHORDAN'S RIVER

KENDRA NORMAN-BELLAMY

MOODY PUBLISHERS
CHICAGO

Library of Congress Cataloging-in-Publication Data

Norman-Bellamy, Kendra.
    Crossing Jhordan's river / Kendra Norman-Bellamy.
      p. cm.
    ISBN-13: 978-0-8024-1255-3
    ISBN-10: 0-8024-1255-6
      1. Suicide victims—Family relationships—Fiction.
    2. Maternal deprivation—Fiction. 3. Husbands—Fiction.
    I. Title.

PS3614.O765C76 2005
813'.6—dc22

                                                      2005000882

ISBN: 0-8024-1255-6
ISBN-13: 978-0-8024-1255-3

1 3 5 7 9 10 8 6 4 2

Printed in the United States of America

CONTENTS

ACKNOWLEDGMENTS

*"In every thing give thanks: for this is the
will of God in Christ Jesus concerning you."*
(1 Thessalonians 5:18)

Thank You, Jesus, for being my Lord and Savior.
Thank You for my king, **Jonathan** and my
princesses, **Brittney** and **Crystal**. Thank You for my parents, **Bishop H.H. & Mrs. Francine Norman**, and my siblings, **Crystal, Harold, Cynthia,** and **Kimberly**. Thank
You for my extended families in the **Holmeses** and the
Bellamys. Thank You for my godparents, **Aunt Joyce** and
Uncle Irvin, and for my godchildren, **Mildred, Jon-Jon,
Courtney,** and **LaMonte**. Thank You for the vision and
reality of **KNB Publications, LLC,** and for **Jamill, Shunda,**
and **Booking Matters, Inc.** Thank You for the sisterhood
of **Circle of Friends II Book Club** and for the many other **book clubs** and **readers** that have supported me. Thank
You for the timeless friendships of **Heather, Gloria,** and
Deborah. Thank You for my literary heroine, **Maya,** my
literary mentors, **Victoria** and **Jacquelin,** and my literary
motivators, **S. James, Travis, Vanessa, Patricia, Stephanie,**

Tia, and **Maurice.** Thank You for my editor, **Cynthia,** and the entire **Moody family.** Thank You for my agent, **Carlton,** and publicists, **Rhonda** and **Terrance.** Thank You for the undying memories of **Jimmy Lee** and those of **Elder Clinton & Mrs. Willie Mae Bellamy.** Thank You for the encouragement of **Pastor Wayne & Mrs. Michelle Mack.** Thank You for **Brian,** whose ballads overpower any threat of writer's block, and for **Fred,** whose gospel beats help me get my praise on at the completion of each manuscript. Finally, Lord, thank You for this **gift** You've given me and for allowing me to give it back to You. It is in Your name that I give thanks for all of these and other blessings. Amen.

THE COLDEST WINTER EVER

Tossing the basketball from hand to hand between sprints, Jhordan Adams, or, as his family affectionately called him, Dano, was in a jovial mood as he headed toward his house. He'd beat his own record during the track-and-field after school practice session today, and he easily qualified for the meet that was scheduled to be held immediately following the holiday break. Dano could hardly wait for dinnertime when he would share the good news with his family.

Meanwhile, he had the rare opportunity of having the house all to himself for a while. His sisters would be getting fitted for new dresses that the next-door neighbor was making them for Christmas. His father had told him early that morning that he and his mother would be at the market shopping when he got home from his after-school activities. For Dano, that meant he could watch whatever he wanted on television and have the freedom of a bathroom visit without interruption.

With him being the youngest child, controlling the television was out of the question, and when everybody was at home, it was a battle for him to get into the bathroom when he needed to. His family only had one, and somebody was always in it. Today was a good day to have the facilities to himself; all of the water he'd drunk during and after practice today was beginning to weigh heavily on his bladder.

Finding the key in its usual storage place under the large rock beneath the porch, Dano bounced up the steps and let himself in. He unloaded his backpack from his shoulders and headed straight to the bathroom that his six-member family shared.

"Mama!" Dano yelled as he stopped in midstride.

His mother looked at him and smiled. His intrusion hadn't even startled her, and his cry didn't change her position or her intentions.

He continued to call out to her. His frantic screams echoed throughout the house. Unfortunately, the only people in the small, well-built wooden structure were the two of them.

"Get out of here, Dano." His mother finally spoke. Her voice was calm, but her eyes were wide and wild—like those of a madwoman.

"Mama!"

"Go out on the porch and wait for your papa."

"Mama, please don't."

"I'm sorry. I have to, baby," the smiling woman said. "I'm doing this for you. *You're* the reason, Dano."

"No, Mama. Please, please, please," the twelve-year-old boy begged through tears as he inched closer to his mother, who sat on the floor by the commode just fifteen feet from where he stood.

"Stay back, Dano," she warned as she held out her unoccupied hand. "You're Mama's big man. You'll be fine. Your papa will be fine. Your sisters will be fine. Everybody will be just fine," she said in an almost melodious tone. "Nobody needs me or wants me anymore. I'm freeing you all. I love you, Dano."

Mustering all of his energies, the frenzied boy lunged forward. He could outrun all of the other boys in his seventh-grade class. His teacher said that he'd one day be a track star and break Carl Lewis's American and Olympic records. Despite the earned first-place ribbons that validated the quickness of his legs, Dano wasn't fast enough to reach his deranged mother, who was holding a gun to her head. The next sound he heard was the ear-piercing blast of the gun, which sent blood and brains splattering against the bathroom walls and on Dano's face and clothes.

"No!" he screamed. She couldn't hear him. It was over. His mother was dead, and all he could do was stand there helplessly while his body fluids ran uncontrollably down his pants leg.

How could she do this? It was almost Christmas. Though the skies were clear and the weather was warm outside, for the little boy who had witnessed it all, it was the coldest winter ever.

For days, even months, he couldn't sleep in peace. Every time he closed his eyes, he could see the look in hers. He could hear the blast of the gun and smell the fresh blood. Many nights, Dano would wake up trembling from the cold sweat that covered his body.

"It wasn't your fault, baby brother," his sisters would

constantly assure him on those days when they'd see him standing alone and staring at nothing in particular.

"It wasn't your fault, son," his father would say while patting his shoulder firmly as his son stared at the dinner plate of food that he couldn't eat.

"It wasn't your fault, Dano," the schoolteachers would tell him when he refused to participate in sporting events and other school activities that he'd once loved.

He wanted to believe them, but she'd told him that he was the reason, and in his head her voice rang louder than theirs. His mother said that she loved him—but if she loved him, why would she do such a thing?

Family, friends, neighbors—they all knew of Lizza's depression and her erratic behavior. She'd be distant and withdrawn one minute and callous and irate the next. Everyone knew, but no one expected her to do anything as drastic as taking her own life.

The man who had been the children's only emotionally stable parent for about as long as they could remember stood with a face void of expression on the day that they buried his wife of seventeen years.

Napoleon was strong and arrogant. He refused to allow his children to see the grief that gripped his heart—but they knew. For weeks, at nightfall following dinner, he'd send his four children outside so that he could release the tears that he'd valiantly held inside him all day.

His three daughters would sit on the bottom step of the front porch and look silently at one another as though not knowing whether or not they should speak. His only son would walk to the pier that was situated more than a hundred feet from their home and cry. Like his father, he was too proud to let his sisters see his anguish.

The house, void of his mother's presence, had been scrubbed and repainted by friends of his father's to cover the blood that had been tracked from the bathroom to the front door as her body was removed. Still, for Dano, the house was a constant reminder of that tragic day.

He hated coming home from school and walking back into the place that immediately caused images to resurface even years later. But Napoleon refused to move. With his own calloused hands and the sweat of his brow he'd helped to build the home for his family after the birth of their firstborn and would not hear of living elsewhere.

The happy boyhood memories that Dano had of growing up in the home that he shared with his parents and three older sisters were all but forgotten. As the years passed, his tears turned to anger toward the woman who chose to leave him motherless, and he vowed that as soon as he was able, he'd move far, far away from the memories of her horrible act of selfishness.

1

What Looks Like Crazy

Kelli sat up and looked at the space beside her. The pillow was neatly in its place, and the covers were too tidy to have been slept on or under. By now, she should be accustomed to the routine, but it never got any easier. At this point in her life, she didn't expect to be sleeping alone.

By anyone's definition, she was still a newlywed. It had been less than a year since she and Jhordan Adams had tied the knot, and it didn't take a rocket scientist to know that they had a *problem*. At twenty-nine, it was her first marriage. Jhordan was only a year older than she, but the marriage was his second.

During their yearlong courtship, he'd been nothing short of a gentleman. The tall, handsome man with the strong features of Tyson Beckford and the deep chocolate skin of Wesley Snipes walked into her church one Sunday morning and took a seat right next to her. Not once during the entire service did Kelli's heart stop pounding.

In a matter of months, she was madly in love, and she knew he felt the same. Jhordan was distant at first and almost seemed to fight his growing affections for her, but fate won the battle. After marrying him, Kelli moved from her one-bedroom apartment in Jackson, Mississippi, to the two-bedroom apartment he rented in the tourist-attraction city of Biloxi. The move was a good one. It placed her closer to her church and her parents.

Kelli had no idea what was wrong. Wesley and Mary Jenkins had raised her to be a very respectable lady. Her parents had been married for nearly forty years—forty *good* years—and she knew how a woman should treat her husband, but apparently she wasn't doing something right.

In the ten months that she'd been married to Jhordan, she could count on both hands the number of times they'd been intimate. When they were together, she enjoyed it immensely. It was as though Jhordan would hold out until he could hold out no longer. He'd be passionate and thorough in his loving of her, but afterward, he'd return to his distant state. At times, the occasional affection, despite its amazement, made her feel like a glorified call girl.

Kelli slipped from under the covers to say her morning prayer. Concentrating was hard. She fought a thousand thoughts as she tried to meditate on God. Questions that she constantly fought flooded her mind. She'd been taught by her parents never to question God, so instead she questioned herself. *Is Jhordan seeing someone else? Does he regret marrying me? Does he love me? What am I doing wrong?*

Shaking the negative thoughts, Kelli struggled to finish her prayer and returned to a seated position on her bed. She *knew* Jhordan loved her, and he *couldn't* be cheating. He wouldn't do that to her. Jhordan was a God-fearing man, and he had good morals and high regard for family. He *wouldn't* dare be so cruel.

"Ms. Kelli?" Kelli heard the muffled voice through her bedroom door followed by a light knock.

"Come on in, sweetie," Kelli said.

The door slowly opened, and her seven-year-old stepdaughter walked in clutching the teddy bear that she had bought her for her birthday just two months ago.

"Good morning," Kelli said.

"Good morning," Jazmin replied with a smile.

Jazmin was a pretty little girl with beautiful dark eyes and a head full of thick, coarse hair that Kelli kept in neat braids to avoid combing it on a daily basis. She was the spitting image of her father and shared both his dimpled chin and his island accent.

Jhordan was born and raised in the Caribbean. San Fernando, Trinidad, was the place he still called home in spite of the fact that he hadn't lived there in eleven years. Though she was born in New York, Jazmin had been raised solely by her father for nearly five years, and very little, if any, of her mother's northern accent could be detected.

His life in Trinidad and his short-lived first marriage were two things that Jhordan seldom discussed voluntarily. He had three older sisters whom Kelli had never met. They all still lived in or near his home country. He spoke favorably of each of them as well as his father. Kelli anxiously looked forward to February when she would get to meet her in-laws for the first time. Jhordan promised to take her to Trinidad during what he referred to simply as Carnival.

Kelli invitingly patted the mattress in front of her and

helped Jazmin climb onto the comforter. She kissed the little girl's forehead and ran her fingers through her fresh braids. She couldn't imagine loving a child more had she given birth to her.

"You hungry?" Kelli asked. "You want some breakfast?"

"Can I have some Honeycomb?" Jazmin asked. It was her favorite cereal. Sometimes she ate it straight out of the box as a snack.

"Sure," Kelli answered.

"Was there a fire?" Jazmin asked while looking at the empty space where she knew her daddy should be.

Though it had only happened once so far in their marriage, Jhordan's job as a fireman at Biloxi Fire Station No. 5 could possibly take him away unexpectedly, so her question was a valid one. It wasn't totally impossible that he'd had an emergency call, but Kelli was certain that he would have left a note if he had.

"I don't think so, sweetie," she answered, trying to be honest without showing her displeasure at his absence. "I think Daddy's just gone to get his hair cut, or maybe he went to the gym to lift some weights this morning. He'll be home soon."

Satisfied with the answer, Jazmin tucked her teddy bear under her arm and slid from the bed.

"I'm gonna wash my face and get dressed," she announced on her way out of the room. "Then I'll be ready to eat. Okay?"

"Okay."

Kelli smiled as the door closed behind her. Jazmin was such a sweet girl. She was a straight-A student in her second-grade class at Carrollton Elementary School and she and Kelli had gotten along wonderfully from the first time they met.

Admittedly, Kelli had been a bit nervous when Jazmin had gone to spend the summer with her mother only four months into her and Jhordan's marriage. She feared that the woman she'd never met would fill the child's head with vicious lies that would turn her against her new step-mother. Jazmin, however, returned seemingly unfazed.

The child had especially been a point of apprehension for Kelli's mother. Mary Jenkins had been adamant when warning Kelli of marrying a man with ties to an ex-wife.

"That girl means that he will always have to deal with a woman he used to love," Mary told her. "You keep that in mind if you decide to marry that man. Now, I ain't got nothing against Jhordan," she quickly clarified. "He seems nice enough. But you're marrying a man with baggage, and I suggest you find out what's in every piece of that baggage before you go flouncing down some church aisle talking 'bout some 'I do.'"

Kelli and her mother had butted heads about several subjects over the years, but maybe this time Mary had been right. She knew very little about Jhordan's previous marriage other than the fact that it hadn't worked out. It seemed to be a touchy subject that he didn't care to go into details about. She'd been unfaithful, he'd said. Kelli could see that it was a sore spot with him, and she didn't push the issue. Now, as she passed the spot that once again hadn't been slept in, she wondered if she'd made a mistake that she'd regret the rest of her life.

Both she and Jazmin had finished their bowls of cereal and were sprawled on the living room floor watching cartoons when the front door opened. Quickly losing interest in the characters on the television screen, Jazmin vacated her spot and ran to greet him.

"Hey, pumpkin," Jhordan said as he lifted her from the floor and embraced her tightly in his arms.

"Daddy, where you been?" she asked. "Did somebody's house get burned down?"

"No," Jhordan said as he released her. "I had to take care of some business."

"Oh," Jazmin said. The answer was enough for her, but not for her stepmother.

Take care of some business? Kelli thought. *Does this 'business' have a name?*

"Hey," Jhordan spoke to her while stepping over her feet and heading to the bedroom.

Kelli didn't immediately respond. If she opened her mouth, she felt as though the wrong words would come out. She didn't want to chance starting a disagreement in front of Jazmin.

"I'll be back in a minute, sweetie," Kelli told her.

Getting up from her seated position on the floor, she followed Jhordan into the bedroom—closing the door behind her.

"Where have you been?" she asked.

His back had been turned to her as he peeled off his dress shirt, leaving him wearing a sleeveless undershirt. He turned to face her. Jhordan was a stunning man. At six feet four, he was one inch shy of standing a full foot taller than his wife.

"Why are you asking me that?" he said. His native tongue had always been mesmerizing to Kelli. Even as she came dangerously close to the line of being angry with him, the sound of his voice weakened her knees.

"Because I want to know," she whispered. "Don't you think I *deserve* to know?"

"Didn't you hear me tell Jazmin that—"

"You had to take care of business, yes," Kelli completed the sentence for him. "What business, Jhordan?" she asked. "I woke up at 4:00 this morning, and you weren't here. When I woke up an hour and a half later, you weren't here. Then when I got up at 8:00, you still weren't here. When did you leave, and how much of your time did this *business* require? This doesn't look like right to me. This looks like crazy."

"What looks like crazy?"

"*This* looks like crazy," Kelli said, becoming more upset that he'd avoided her question. "Where have you been?" she repeated her earlier probe.

"Why are you questioning me?" Jhordan asked.

"Why aren't you answering me?"

"I slept in my truck, Kelli," Jhordan said. His impatience was clear in his tone. "I didn't mean to. I just went for a drive around 2:00 this morning and parked. I fell asleep, and when I woke up, it was 8:30."

"Why did you go for a drive at 2:00 in the morning?"

"Don't you ever need time alone, Kelli?" It was apparent from his expression that Jhordan didn't appreciate the cross-examination he was receiving.

"Baby, we haven't been married quite ten months yet," Kelli said. "*Ten* months, Jhordan," she repeated. "No, there's not a time that I want to be alone. I want to be with you. But you know what? I *feel* more alone now than I ever did before I married you."

Kelli wished that she could put ten seconds back on the game clock and have a chance at a do-over. But she knew she couldn't take the words back. Jhordan stood silently and stared at her before walking into the closet and hanging his shirt on the line. Still quiet, he walked past her and toward the room door. Before turning the knob to walk out, he faced her once more.

"If the man God made me to be isn't good enough for you," he said, "you're free to go. It won't be the first time it's happened to me," Jhordan added. "I'll survive."

Immediately upon the door's closing, tears flooded Kelli's eyes. She couldn't believe the words she'd just heard. Climbing back into the bed and burying her face into her pillow, she wept.

2

SECOND SUNDAY

Sunday morning's service was in full swing by the time Jhordan parked his black Toyota Tundra in the nearly full parking lot of the nondenominational church where he and his family worshiped. As he walked between the parked cars on his way toward the entrance doors, Jhordan stopped beside his wife's car. Through the passenger window, he could see a photo of himself in the cup holder near the armrest.

How could he question her love for him? Deep down he knew that Kelli had a right as his wife to question him. He'd given her every right to be upset. Jhordan knew that his inability to trust and his inability to totally give his heart to a woman was a spiritual and mental battle that he'd fought almost all of his life.

He loved Kelli more than he was willing to admit—even more than he wanted to love her. He'd promised himself after his farce of a marriage to Sadonia that he'd never love again. Then three years later, Kelli walked into his life and changed everything.

He remembered the first time he laid eyes on her at this very same church. Jhordan became distracted during worship when he noticed her in the seat beside him. Her hair, streaked with soft brown highlights, hung to her shoulders, and her teal sweater dress seemed tailor-made just for her.

"Hi, I'm Jhordan Adams," he said, smiling as he introduced himself following the benediction.

Kelli's smile was hypnotizing.

What a name, she thought, eyeing this handsome man she'd never seen at church before. *Sounds so distinguished.* She sized him up and guessed that he might be a lawyer or something corporate.

"I'm Kelli. It's good meeting you. Are you a visitor?" Giving her first name was good enough.

"Yeah, and I'll definitely be back."

The more Jhordan got to know her, the more he found himself attracted to Kelli. Initially, though, he had fought hard against the mounting feelings that he had for her. Before her, Jhordan had no problem fighting off emotional attachments to even the most eye-catching women. Kelli, however, not only caught his eye with her beautiful mocha skin and well-designed body—but her quiet demeanor and sweet disposition caught his heart.

Throughout their twelve-month courtship, they'd been committed to abstaining from any physical contact other than hand-holding and innocent pecks on the cheek. Jhordan had never known anyone quite like her, and as loudly as he tried to tell himself not to fall in love with her, his heart wasn't listening. He knew he had to make her his in every way—and the only way to do that was to make her his bride.

Kelli was right. It had been less than a year, and perhaps he shouldn't need time apart from her, but he did. Not because he disliked her or didn't want to be around her, but because if he didn't get time away from her, he'd be consumed by her. Even after committing to her in marriage, he'd told himself that he could be her husband without totally giving his heart to her. He needed to be detached just enough so that if she walked out on him like Sadonia did, his heart wouldn't be shattered into a thousand pieces. That was a street that he did not want to walk down again.

The sounds of hundreds of hands clapping together met Jhordan as he finally walked through the doors of Biloxi Temple. It was the second Sunday—the Sunday that the church videotaped the service for the church's library—the Sunday that the pews were always packed. He took a seat near the rear of the church and scanned the crowd for his wife and daughter, spotting them sitting near his in-laws. Kelli was wearing one of his favorite outfits. The purple A-line dress flattered her shape well.

Jhordan fidgeted in his seat as the sermon entered its second half hour. Pastor Winston Berry was an anointed preacher. He was very overweight but had recently been voted one of the best-dressed men in the state of Mississippi by *The Sun Herald*.

Jhordan had chosen Biloxi Temple by chance on his first visit. Admittedly, he continued coming because of his interest in Kelli, but Pastor Berry's preaching and vision were major reasons that he remained even after he'd succeeded in catching the girl.

Some Sundays, Pastor Berry's messages would be short and sweet. Today wasn't one of those days. Periodically throughout the sermon, one of the elderly missionaries in the corner started shouting. By the forty-five-minute mark, the old lady had shouted so much that her thigh-high stockings had slipped down to the point of becoming footies.

Jhordan glanced at his watch, but not because he wasn't enjoying the sermon. The preacher was ministering an awesome message on love—and loving was what Jhordan was in the mood for. It had been more than three weeks since he'd enjoyed a session of unbridled passion with Kelli. He wasn't oblivious of the result of yesterday's quarrel. He knew that his words had hurt her. The late-morning conversation was the last exchange that they'd had. Jhordan had spent much of the rest of the day in the park with Jazmin while Kelli spent the day at home.

It wasn't until the late evening that he began regretting the way he'd handled the situation. He'd had the whole night, as he worked at the firehouse, to think about what had been said and what had been done. His wife had been right, and his upsetting response wasn't warranted.

If this man tells me to turn to my neighbor and say one more thing!

"Lord, forgive me," Jhordan immediately whispered following his thought.

The sermon had been going on now for fifty-five minutes, and he was tired of looking into the cocked eyes of Sister Emma Jean Matchett and repeating phrase after phrase. The woman appeared to have never visited a dentist in her entire life, and she always needed a breath mint.

To make matters worse, the heating system in the church wasn't working properly. The hot air continued to blow from the vents and would not shut off as it should. They'd even tried turning it off by hand, but the heat continued to blow. The opened windows were the only reason that the building hadn't reached the point of sweltering.

Last Sunday, the same problem existed, but they were able to manually control it. This week, even that primitive method didn't work. Pastor Berry had announced last Sunday that a repairman had been called to take care of the problem, but it was more uncomfortable today than it had been then. Though winter had arrived and with Christmas just round the corner it was cold on the outside, the old cement building with so many bodies inside felt like a closed coffin.

Jhordan glanced across the aisle at Kelli. She was using a handkerchief to wipe the sweat from her face. The hairs from her bangs were beginning to stick to her forehead, and her onetime curls at the ends of her hair were all but nonexistent. Her hair spray generally held up well in adverse conditions, but apparently Miss Clairol had never been tested at Biloxi Temple on a second Sunday with the central heating and air on the blink.

"It's gonna be hotter in hell than it is in here."

The sudden echo of the words briefly broke Jhordan from his thoughts. He turned to his left and looked in Sister Matchett's face once more. The lady dipped her head to the side as though telling him off as she said the words. Jhordan noticed that everyone else was looking at one another and saying the words too. Obviously, he'd missed yet another "turn to your neighbor" moment.

"Say amen, somebody," Pastor Berry said as he finally closed his Bible.

"Amen!" the congregation obeyed.

Twenty minutes later, after all of the announcements and the benediction had been given, Jhordan made his way through the dispersing crowd toward his family.

"Jhordan." Wesley Jenkins, his father-in-law, greeted him with a firm handshake. "Glad you could make it this morning."

"Thanks, Mr. Jenkins," Jhordan said. He quickly searched the man's face to see if there was any indication that Kelli had discussed their argument with him. His genuine smile implied that he wasn't aware.

"Hey, baby," Mary Jenkins said as she pulled his face to her and planted a kiss on his cheek.

His mother-in-law had finally accepted him. He knew that she hadn't been too thrilled when Kelli told them that she was dating Jhordan. Although she no longer lived at home, when he decided to pop the question, Jhordan respectfully asked Wesley for his daughter's hand. Her father seemed genuinely happy as he sealed his permission with a warm embrace of his future son-in-law. It was obvious that Mary wasn't as enthused, but over the months she'd slowly been convinced that Jhordan had matters with Sadonia under control.

"Daddy!" Jhordan opened his arms just in time to catch his excited little girl upon her notice of his approach.

"Hey, sweetheart," he said as he returned her heartwarming hug.

"You had to put out some fires?" she asked.

"Just one," Jhordan said.

He eased the girl onto the floor and walked toward Kelli, who was finishing a conversation with her older sister. The two girls were the spitting image of their parents. Cheryl was long and lean just like her father, and she shared his same heavy eyebrows and full lips. She was attractive in her own way but couldn't hold a candle to Kelli, in Jhordan's opinion.

Like her mother, Kelli was short in stature and, in the words of one of Jhordan's coworkers following a visit that Kelli had made to the fire station a few months ago, "fine to death." She was heavier than her size 2, pencil-thin sister, but all of the weight fell in the right places.

"Hey," Jhordan said guardedly as he stood next to her.

"Hey." She tried to smile, but Jhordan knew that her thoughts were still on yesterday's heated conversation that had turned ugly.

"Y'all coming to Mama's for dinner?" Cheryl asked, unaware of the tension between the two of them.

"No," Jhordan quickly answered before Kelli could. "We're going out."

"I want to go and play with the babies," Jazmin whined.

Cheryl and her husband, Tony, were the proud parents of three-year-old twins, Christopher and Tonya. To Jazmin, they were like the siblings that she didn't yet have, and she loved playing big sister to them.

"Let her come," Cheryl urged. "We'll bring her home later."

"It's a school night," Kelli started.

"That's fine," Jhordan interrupted. "You all can take her."

"Yea!" Jazmin cheered.

"I guess we'll see y'all later, then," Cheryl said just before taking Jazmin's hand and walking toward the exit.

"You know every time she goes with them they bring her home late," Kelli said. "She may miss her bedtime."

"I know," Jhordan said while slipping his arm around her waist. "Today, I'll make an exception," he said. "We need to talk."

3

TROUBLE MAN

Number eleven could possibly have been Jhordan's best work yet, but somehow it didn't bring the satisfaction that being with him once had. The experience was incredible while it lasted, but Kelli had been there before—ten times before—and she knew that after all the lovemaking had ended, he would rebuild a mile-long stretch of freeway between them, and she'd once again feel lonely.

Jhordan had always had his moments where he seemed distant, even when they dated, but it had magnified times ten since they'd married. In all honesty, her husband was one of the most appealing men she'd ever met. Physically, she couldn't ask for more. The word *sexy* barely described him justly. He was everything a woman could hope for, but his attributes didn't stop with his appearance. Even spiritually, his life seemed solid. Praying and reading Scriptures were a part of his daily routine, and he loved attending church weekly—even if he had to come straight from work.

However, in spite of all of that, he seemed to be struggling mentally, and she felt as though she were a factor in the equation that he was battling with. Kelli didn't want to believe that there could be another woman in Jhordan's life, but his constant need for space certainly gave her reason to ponder the possibility.

Five years ago—even three years ago—Kelli would have never imagined herself being married to Jhordan. He didn't match the criteria that she'd conjured up in her mind when she graduated high school and enrolled in college. In some ways, he was more than she anticipated and in other ways, he fell short.

She'd thought that her ideal mate would be an average-looking man. Nice looking—but not so handsome that he'd stand out in a crowd or turn the heads of other women. In that area, Jhordan exceeded her expectations. The first time she met him, she remembered thinking that even he could hear the beating of her heart inside her chest. Though he was exceptionally good-looking, the fact that he wasn't conceited or self-centered attracted her the most.

On the professional end, Jhordan didn't measure up to her self-set standards. Kelli had verbalized on several occasions that her soul mate would be a college graduate with a degree that qualified him for a job of prominence. He'd be anything from a college professor to a medical doctor. Jhordan never attended college, but she was proud of his noble profession. He was a hardworking man, and her love for him had erased all of the things that she deemed as shortcomings.

As Kelli drove to work, she clicked on her radio and

sang along with Yolanda Adams as she declared, "The battle is not yours; it's the Lord's."

Kelli hoped Sasha would not work her nerves, especially this morning.

"Good morning, Mrs. Jhordan Adams," Sasha, her assistant, sang as she greeted Kelli at the doorway of Racks of Reading. The woman had a knack for conjuring up descriptive middle names to fit whomever it was she was talking to or about.

Kelli had opened the bookstore four years ago after graduating from the University of Mississippi with a bachelor of arts degree in elementary education. With a love for words and well-written books, she immediately jumped at the chance to teach reading classes at one of the local schools. Nevertheless, things didn't work out as she had hoped.

One year in the public school system was more than enough for her. She'd always heard that in order to be a good teacher, one must do it for the love of the job and not for the financial benefits—especially since it didn't pay all that well. After taking on a class of sixth graders for one school term, Kelli agreed.

The job birthed a host of feelings inside of her, but love wasn't one of them. Instead, the children's constant behavior problems made her want to throw up her hands and just walk out. So, she admitted defeat, bowed out gracefully, and found a new way to enjoy and share her love for reading.

Best friends for the past seven years, Sasha Gray and Kelli had been college roommates. Sasha withdrew at the beginning of her junior year to marry her high school sweetheart who had taken leave from his assignment in the Navy to pop the question.

A loud and bubbly red-headed white girl from

Roanoke, Alabama, Sasha and Kelli seemed to have very little, if anything, in common. Yet, somehow during those late nights of studying in their dorm room, they'd become the best of friends. When Kelli decided to go into business, her college friend had been her first and only choice for her assistant manager.

"Good morning," Kelli responded.

With all that they had shared and as close as she and Sasha were, Kelli couldn't bring herself to reveal the disappointments that had surfaced in her still young marriage. Sasha and her husband, Craig, had the perfect union. They were apart a lot as he traveled and served, but when they were together they were one of the happiest couples that Kelli knew. There was no way Sasha would be able to relate to her situation with Jhordan.

"How's that Island cutie of yours?"

"He's fine," Kelli answered.

"Yes, he is," Sasha said with a laugh as she headed to a bookshelf to replenish the dwindled inventory.

Racks of Reading was a small but flourishing store. Sales had increased with each year of the store's existence. Aside from books, magazines, and Bibles, she also sold floral arrangements that were handmade by Sasha, scented candles, fragrances for men and women, stuffed animals, and snack items.

"Girl, people are still talking about your wedding," Sasha said as she joined Kelli at the counter. "Did I tell you I had the picture blown up that y'all took right after the ceremony? You and Jhordan look so good together in that one," she added with a giggle.

"Yes, you told me," Kelli said. "Do we have any more copies of Bernice McFadden's latest novel in stock?" Kelli said, quickly changing the subject. "We received a fax from a book club, and they need twelve copies."

"I'll take a look," Sasha said as she disappeared into the storage room.

Kelli sighed and then quickly put on her best smile to greet two regular customers who had come in and were headed to the selection of children's books on the reduced-price table.

Following yesterday's service, she and Jhordan had enjoyed dinner at a nearby seafood restaurant that they often frequented. They talked about the disagreement that they'd had, and Jhordan had apologized for the open invitation that he had extended for her to abandon the marriage. She wanted to believe that the apology was genuine, but all the while he spoke to her, she could see the desire in his eyes.

Kelli knew from the moment that he'd turned down Cheryl's invitation for them to join the family for dinner that he wanted to be alone with her. She wasn't complaining. God knows she'd wanted to be in Jhordan's arms for weeks, and knowing that he finally wanted the same was a wonderful feeling. But she also knew that the warmth and closeness would be short-lived.

He was her husband. She shouldn't be left to feel like a mistress that he used whenever he wanted to satisfy his physical needs. She loved Jhordan dearly and couldn't imagine herself without him, but marriage wasn't supposed to feel like this.

"Hi there."

Kelli looked up from her thoughtful stare at the pages of her record book and into the eyes of a handsome face she'd never seen before.

"Hi," she said. "I'm sorry. I didn't see you standing there. May I help you?"

"Wow," he said as he looked at her in approval. "I'm sure you could."

"Seriously," Kelli said, trying not to show the flattery that she felt. "Were you looking for a particular book or gift?"

"Are you the manager?" he asked.

"I'm the *owner* and manager," Kelli corrected him.

"Wonderful," he said as he extended his hand. "It's always good to see one of our own as a successful entrepreneur. I'm Stuart McMillian. Good to make your acquaintance."

"Kelli Adams," she responded while accepting his hand. "Was there something you were looking for in particular?" she asked again.

"Yes," Stuart said as his eyes fell to the gold band on her left hand, "but I think I came looking just a little too late."

"Mr. McMillian—"

"Please," he said, "call me Stuart."

"Stuart," Kelli began again, "we have a large selection of books and gift items. If you'd like to browse, please feel free to do so, and if you have any questions, my assistant or I will be glad to help you."

"Thank you," he said with a sly smile. "I'll take a look around."

Kelli tried to appear uninterested as he slowly walked away from her desk to one of the nearby bookshelves. Stuart was tall, lean, and strikingly handsome. He was what her mother would call "high yella"—but his eyes were dark and mysterious, and his sense of style was impeccable. The suit he wore appeared expensive and custom-made, and in it he looked like new money.

Turning her eyes away, Kelli returned to staring at the pages of the record-keeping book. Sasha emerged from the storage room with an armload of books and rounded the corner.

"We had exactly a dozen," she announced while placing the books on the back counter. "If you want me to, I'll go ahead and order more."

Kelli's unresponsiveness caught her full attention. Sasha stood next to her and watched her momentarily as she mindlessly looked at the blank page of paper.

"Hellooooo?"

"Huh?" Kelli turned to face her assistant.

"Well, where were *you?*" Sasha asked. "Your mind was a million miles away. I was talking, and you weren't even listening to me. Why are you staring at that page like there's even any writing on it? What's the matter?"

"Nothing." Kelli shrugged. "I guess I was just thinking about—"

"Jhordan—I know," Sasha said with a knowing nod of her head. "Look, you ain't even got to explain. I was a newlywed once too, you know. I know how wonderfully intense those first few months can be." Sasha gave a sly grin.

"Congratulations."

Both women turned and faced Stuart as he approached the counter once more.

"You're a newlywed," he said with a smile. "This Jhordan is quite the lucky man."

Sasha looked from Stuart to Kelli in confusion.

"This is Mr. Stuart McMillian," Kelli introduced the two. "He came in to browse."

"Any new customer of ours is good people," Sasha said with a grin, shaking Stuart's outstretched hand. "I'm sorry that I was talking so loud," she said. "I didn't intend to let the whole store in on my and Kelli's conversation."

"No harm done," Stuart said. He placed an *Ebony* magazine and a pack of crackers on the counter in front of Kelli as he spoke. "You have some very nice things in your store," he said. "I'll have to come back when I have more time to shop."

"Thank you," Kelli said as she handed him his receipt and change.

"Here's my card," Stuart said. He pulled a shiny sterling silver business card holder from his pocket and handed a card to both of them. "If you ever need my services—"

"You're a lawyer," Sasha observed. "Oh," she added quickly, "you're one of *those* McMillians."

"My condolences," Kelli added. "One of the partners of your company passed away a few months ago, as I recall."

"Yes," Stuart flashed a smile as though pleased that she'd remembered. "Rayford McMillian was my uncle—my father's brother. He died in June. I just moved here from Atlanta eight weeks ago to take his place in the family business. My moving here was my father's idea," he further explained. "I've only been practicing for a year, but I'm holdin' it down. Hang on to that card in case you need my services."

"Thank you," Sasha said as he picked up his bag and prepared to walk away.

"I specialize in divorces," he added with a grin before turning and disappearing on the other side of the exit door.

The two women watched until he disappeared around the corner toward the parking lot. It seemed that Sasha could barely wait for him to be out of sight.

"Did you see how he looked at you when he said that?" Her voice had taken on a pitch two octaves higher than normal. "I *know* he didn't," she continued. "Jhordan will bust a cap in his . . . Girl, he must don't know," she rambled. "Jhordan's got more muscles in one of his arms than he got in his whole body. You just wait. I'm gonna tell him."

"No, you're not, Sasha," Kelli said. "We are not in middle school, and you're not going to try and start a playground fight."

"But he looked right at you, Kelli. I can smell trouble a mile away," she added, "and that's a trouble man if I've ever smelled one."

"So what?" Kelli said as she crumpled Stuart's business card and dropped it in the garbage can. "I can handle my own, okay? Chances are we won't see him again anyway."

"This is what I think of your services, Mr. Home-Wrecker McMillian," Sasha said while angrily ripping the card in small pieces and dropping them in the can with Kelli's. "You're cute," she said, speaking into the can as though the shredded paper could hear her scolding, "but you ain't *that* cute."

4

MEN CRY
IN THE DARK

From his Lake Pointe Avenue apartment to Mount
Nebo Christian Church was less than eight miles.
Jhordan knew the toll that his issues were having on his
marriage, and for the past three months, he'd been seek-
ing help at the downtown Biloxi church. He enjoyed dinner with Kelli and Jazmin, waited until his daughter had
gone to bed, and then left despite his wife's protesting.

Jamison T. Ellis, D.D., was the pastor of the popular
church and had allowed Jhordan to come to him for late-
night counseling. In Jhordan's mind, most men couldn't
come close to understanding his dilemma, but if he was
going to talk to one, it definitely wouldn't be one who
knew his wife. Pastor Berry knew Kelli, and the two of
them had a history that dated back to their high school
days when they'd dated for a brief time. Jhordan wouldn't
feel comfortable discussing his past or his present with
him. He respected Pastor Berry as a preacher, but he

couldn't confide in him. Because of it, twice a month Jhordan and Dr. Ellis would meet, and Dr. Ellis would try, though with little success, to get to the root of Jhordan's troubles.

Because the details were still painful, Jhordan had only exposed portions of the sordid story that had brought him to the place where he was in life. Attending church more often seemed to be Dr. Ellis's answer to everything. In Jhordan's opinion, if attending church was the answer, his problem would have been rectified long ago.

He'd accepted Christ eight years ago while living in Queens, New York. It was in that church that he'd met Sadonia. The Singles for Christ Ministry meetings had at one time been an enjoyable time of fellowship for him. There, he'd met a lot of people who could relate to the issues that non-married Christians like himself faced.

That particular meeting was held at a local restaurant. The small crew had been gathered at a long table in the back corner of Steak & Ale, chatting and discussing biblical principles with their group leader for quite some time.

Sadonia had chosen that restaurant to dine alone in on the same night. She'd sat at a nearby table and overheard the conversations that were taking place at the table where he sat with about eight others. Noticing her interest in their topic of discussion, the pastor invited her to join them. She sat right next to Jhordan and instantly captured his interest. Little did he know that she was fresh out of a long-term relationship that would eventually lead to the demise of their love affair.

It was the beginning of a brief dating period that lasted only a few weeks and led to a marriage where the blissfulness didn't endure much longer than the courtship. The wedding was beautiful, though. Sadonia wore a gown that drew gasps from both the audience and her groom when she came walking down the aisle. When they walked out hand in hand following the nuptials, there was a gold stretch limousine waiting to whisk them away. It was the stuff dreams were made of. Little did Jhordan know that this dream would end like a horrific nightmare.

They were married just a few months before troubling situations began to surface that raised questions in Jhordan's mind. By the middle of that December, a few weeks past their first anniversary, the marriage began to head in a downward spiral. It still haunted Jhordan every time he thought of Sadonia. Because of Sadonia's unfaithfulness, he regretted that he'd ever put his heart in her hands.

Running had become his answer for everything. A year following his bitter divorce, Jhordan left New York and headed south—ultimately settling in Mississippi. Through a miracle that he would have never expected, Sadonia abruptly gave up her parental rights, which gave Jhordan full custody of their toddler.

The man that Sadonia had left him for told her in no uncertain terms that he didn't want to care for another man's child. When given the choice to live the good life married to the rich stockbroker or a mediocre life with her daughter, Sadonia chose the money.

Ultimately, life for Sadonia came full circle. Two years later, the man she'd chosen over Jazmin left her for someone else that he'd been secretly seeing when he made business trips—just as she had done Jhordan. It crushed her. She'd tried to regain custody, but the courts refused her request. When she tried to regain Jhordan's heart, he'd denied her as well. Jhordan knew that Sadonia regretted the decision that she'd made to abandon both him and their child, but he could find no sympathy in his heart for her.

Now, years later, Dr. Jamison T. Ellis, the well-respected pastor of Mount Nebo, was trying to get Jhordan more involved in church activities in order to solve what his involvement in a church activity had caused. Jhordan declined with the silent shaking of his head.

"I'm not talking about a ministry for single people," Dr. Ellis explained. "I'm talking about a gathering of men, just like you, who are battling with one situation or another. No one is there to judge you, Brother Adams. Everyone is there for the same reason. Women will discuss things in an open forum, but *men cry in the dark*. This is a way for men to release themselves of burdens that they'd otherwise carry with them to the grave."

As he listened to the pastor's ongoing pleas, Jhordan's mind wandered back to one of the meetings at his New York church. He remembered listening as several of the group members expressed desires to be married and those things that they felt a woman or man should have to offer in a marriage. Thinking back, he almost laughed at the remembrance of hearing one of the sisters express how much a woman valued an ambitious, responsible, and honest man. His experience told him otherwise.

Before he married Sadonia, Jhordan would have wholeheartedly agreed. At the singles' meetings he used to actively participate by giving his view on matters when the floor was opened for comments. He was proud and thankful of the way his father had raised him. Napoleon Adams, though not a churchgoing man, preached to his only son how to treat a woman as a gift. It was the way he'd treated Jhordan's mother.

Jhordan used to be so sure of himself, realizing that he had all those qualities that he thought a Christian woman would want and could appreciate. Now with a disastrous marriage and a dead mother to his credit, he no longer knew what a woman wanted, and the last thing he needed was to be surrounded by a bunch of men who had fallen into the same trap that he had.

"Brother Adams," Dr. Ellis was saying, "I know you have your reservations, but at some point you have to totally trust God and move on."

"In other words, you're tired of these meetings with me," Jhordan said defensively.

"No," the pastor refuted. "These meetings are why I'm here. I'm a pastor, and counseling is a part of what I do. God has called me to do it, and my divinity schooling licensed me to do it," he reminded him. "But God has also called me to give you the truth—even if it offends you."

"The truth is not what offends me, Dr. Ellis," Jhordan said. "What offends me is when people tell me to just move on as though all I've endured is a stubbed toe."

"I didn't tell you to simply move on," Dr. Ellis said. "I told you to *trust God* and move on. There's a big difference. My intention is not to treat your life's experiences as an injured toe, but keep in mind that you've chosen to keep most of the details of your past a secret, and therefore I don't know the true depth of your injuries.

"I've also been repeatedly made aware that discussing the details of your marriage to and divorce from the former Mrs. Adams are off-limits," Dr. Ellis pointed out.

Jhordan looked away from the spectacle-wearing pastor and tightened his jaws in an attempt to restrain his tongue. He didn't want to be disrespectful toward him, but he was about to trespass onto grounds that were totally and unquestionably not up for discussion.

"You can relax." Dr. Ellis tried to calm him after taking note of his change in demeanor. "I'm not going to press you on that issue tonight, Brother Adams. But I do want you to know that I am here *if* you ever decide to talk about it—and you really do need to."

"I appreciate that, Dr. Ellis," Jhordan said in poorly masked annoyance. "However, I can assure you that your availability is not warranted."

"Neither is your sarcasm," the pastor said.

Jhordan took in a deep breath and then released it. "I'm sorry," he said.

Dr. Ellis removed his eyeglasses and placed them on the desk in front of him. "I'll waive your remark and accept your apology if you'll give me an honest answer," he said. "Deal?"

Feeling convicted for getting smart with someone who was attempting to help him, it only seemed right to agree to the proposal, though he had a feeling that he'd regret it.

"Deal," Jhordan said.

"Why do you push everybody away?" he asked. "Why do you insist on carrying this burden by yourself? You have a wife who you love and who loves you. Why don't you talk to her instead of pushing her away?"

He'd guessed right. He was beginning to regret it already. Besides, that was three questions.

"Because it's *my* burden," Jhordan answered. "Kelli has nothing to do with this. I brought this on myself, and I will take care of it by myself."

"But you *can't*—don't you see that?" Dr. Ellis told him. "If you could, you wouldn't still be in so much pain after all these years. If you were capable of handling this, you would have erased it by now."

"I think I'm doing well, Pastor," Jhordan said. "I think I'm doing *very* well, considering."

"Considering what?" his pastor challenged.

"Considering all the things that have gone on in my life," he answered.

"That's a general answer," Dr. Ellis said. "That's like me asking you what kind of drink you want, and you tell me you want a soda. There are dozens of sodas on the market. I would need to know what brand in order to give it to you, and I need to know exactly what *things* you're referring to right now in order to help you."

"But I don't want your help." Jhordan tried to remain calm. "I don't *need* your help."

"Then why are you here?"

The silence that followed seemed lengthy and deafening.

"Are you happy, Brother Adams?" Dr. Ellis broke the thick quietness.

"Why shouldn't I be?"

"You're being evasive again. That didn't answer my question."

Jhordan stood silently and looked away. If Dr. Ellis had been anything other than a pastor, he would be less careful of how he reacted and responded to the drilling session. He knew the preacher's intentions were to help, but the details of his life were not points of debate. Jhordan turned back to him in silence. He knew his eyes were cold, but he was in no mood for tonight's lecture.

"I know you want me to let this go," Dr. Ellis said fearlessly, "and I will. But I need you to know that you can't go on like this. I see your rage every time your ex-wife's name is mentioned, and while I understand it, I must challenge you about it.

"Mind you," he continued, "I don't condone her behavior either. Marriage is sacred. She betrayed you, and I know that can't be an easy cross to bear. However, God doesn't hold you responsible for her behavior, but you are responsible for the way you react to it. Don't let the past break you, Brother Adams. Release the pain and, most of all, the *animosity*. Get it out of your heart. You know, the Word tells us that if we regard iniquity in our heart, God will not hear us.

"If you don't talk to me," the pastor said in a pleading tone, "talk to *someone*. Just make sure that person is trustworthy and dependable. Everybody isn't out to deceive you. I don't know the details of your unhealed wounds, but I know that they are deeper than you've let on. Whatever this secret is from your past marriage," he continued, "it's eating you up inside, and that's not good. You have to allow yourself the opportunity to heal. You deserve that, Brother Adams."

Jhordan turned away again.

"Son," the pastor said, "you're a good man. You're a *strong* man. You're a *Christian* man," he stressed. "But you are *only* a man. You're trying to bear the pain all by yourself, but you don't have to. God supplies us with everything we need in our lives, and you need someone to talk to. In your case, your wife deserves to know whatever it is that you're keeping from her."

Jhordan remained silent as Dr. Ellis spoke. How the pastor knew that there were secrets, he didn't know. He'd never talked to anyone about any secret concerning his first marriage or about any pain that he was holding on to. He swallowed hard to tame the tears that threatened to fall.

"If you love her like you say you do," Dr. Ellis continued, "you'll talk to her. How long do you think she'll be able to live with a man who avoids her? When you're away from home—like now—does she even know where you are? If you don't talk to her, you'll lose her. Is that what you want?"

Seeing that he'd struck a tender chord, and not wanting to rehash memories of the past or possibilities of the future any more than he already had, Dr. Ellis shook Jhordan's hand and ended the meeting in prayer. "Lord, we thank You for this time that You've allowed us to be together. Thank You that Your Word is a lamp unto our feet and a light unto our paths. I pray for healing for Jhordan's heart and that You'd give him an even stronger love for his wife. Help me to help him. In Jesus' name."

Finally able to escape, Jhordan released a heavy sigh as the church doors closed behind him. The chilly night air was a welcome and refreshing break from being inside Dr. Ellis's office, where the walls seemed as if they were closing in on him.

Heading toward his truck, he felt a warm tear roll down the side of his face and quickly wiped it away. The interior of his vehicle made him feel secure. For several minutes he sat there in thought. Jhordan's conversation with Dr. Ellis had left him shaken. He couldn't interpret whether he felt angry, fearful, or somehow invaded, but this session seemed more brutal than any in the past.

Seeing the building turn dark and knowing that Dr. Ellis would soon exit the doors, he hastily cranked up his truck and drove away.

5
THE HEART
OF A WOMAN

Wesley and Mary Jenkins had been married for thirty-eight years. Though both their daughters were grown and married, the nest in which they raised them was never empty for long. The proud grandparents had transformed Cheryl's old bedroom into a playroom for their twin grandchildren, whom they looked after on a daily basis while their daughter and son-in-law worked.

Professions in the educational system were common in the Jenkins family. For thirty-five years, Wesley had worked in the transportation department of one school district or another. Until just four years ago, Mary had been employed as the head cook at one of the local elementary schools.

When Cheryl graduated from the University of Mississippi, she returned to the campus as a financial aid administrator. There, she met the man who would ultimately become her husband. Tony was one of the college's most popular instructors in the Applied Science program. He loved his job, and it was evident that his students respected and admired him. When Kelli chose to teach advanced reading at the elementary level, she'd continued the family tradition.

Now retired from driving school buses for the Harrison County School System, Wesley enjoyed spending his days working around the house and entertaining his grandchildren. With another day coming to an end, he sat in front of the television and read the sports section of the *Bay Press*.

"They finally went to sleep," Mary said, entering the room.

"I told you I'd get them so worn out that they wouldn't be able to do nothing else but sleep."

"You a man of your word." Mary laughed while settling on the sofa and kicking off her slippers.

"I think it's time we ask Kelli and Jhordan if they want us to start picking Jazmin up from school in the afternoons," Wesley suggested. They'd had the conversation before. "She can come over here and play with her cousins instead of going into that after-school program 'til Jhordan and Kelli get off from work."

"They're not *really* cousins, Wesley, and the twins don't know her all that well."

"They *are* really cousins, Mary." Wesley folded his paper and looked at her. "Kelli is married to Jhordan, and that makes both him and his daughter family. I can't believe you still saying stuff like that after all this time."

"I don't mean no harm," Mary said. "Jazmin is a nice child, but like I said, Tonya and Christopher don't really know her."

"That's 'cause they don't get much time around her, and we're gonna change that. The little time that she spends with them, the babies enjoy it. I'm sure that Jhordan won't mind. Besides, Jazmin can help us keep an eye on them. Her being here would be as much a help to us as it would be to her parents."

"We'll see," Mary said.

"What's wrong with you?" Wesley asked. "You act like this is a problem or something. You ain't got nothing against Jhordan or his child, do you?"

"The child ain't but seven, Wesley. What could I have against her?"

"And Jhordan?" Wesley pried.

Mary sat silently for a moment as though choosing her words carefully. "He hadn't done nothing either, I don't suppose," she said. "I just get the feeling that something ain't right over there with our baby daughter."

"What do you mean?"

"I mean, she just seems a little sad to me. You haven't noticed? She just don't seem as happy as she was when they first got married. I think there's something that she ain't telling us."

"I hadn't noticed anything," Wesley said.

"Of course you haven't," Mary told him. "You're a man, and men are just not as keen as women are on picking up on these things."

"You mean we ain't as *overdramatic* and don't make up stuff in our minds like y'all do," Wesley said with a chuckle.

"Think about it," Mary said, ignoring his insinuation. "Remember how when they first got married, how she'd be skinning and grinning all the time? When's the last time you saw her beaming like that? And she used to always rush to close the store down and get home. I called up there at 7:30 the day before yesterday, and she was still there."

"What you doing calling the store that time of night?"

"I had called the house, and she wasn't there, so I called her cell phone. Both her and Jazmin was up there at the store. She had closed the store, went and picked up the girl, and then went back to the store to finish some work. That ain't the Kelli Renee Adams that ran that store eight or nine months ago."

Wesley leaned back in his recliner and replayed the past few months in his mind. It was all true. Kelli didn't seem as happy as she had been. When the girls were growing teenagers, they'd always come to him with their problems and concerns—especially Kelli. She'd always been a daddy's girl, and she'd talk to him when she wouldn't talk to her mother. Back then, he never had to try and figure out what was going on in her life.

"Well, when people first get married," he finally spoke, "they're always bouncing off the walls and can't get enough of each other. Like us." Wesley pointed his finger at himself and then toward his wife. "You used to run your fingers through my hair when we sat in the living room together. Now look at us. I'm over here . . . You're over there."

"Plus you ain't got no hair on top now," Mary said with a laugh. "I guess I must've rubbed it all out. Besides that, we been married a long, long time. Jhordan and Kelli are still newlyweds. They shouldn't be tired of each other or even used to each other yet. I'm telling you, Wesley, something's going on over there."

"What's your guess?" Wesley asked.

"I don't know. Jhordan's got an ex-wife who could be meddling in his life. He's always been evasive about his first marriage, and that's the reason that I tried to tell her that marrying him might not be a good idea. I ain't got nothing against him personally, but you don't marry a man who won't lay all his cards out on the table. Then there's the fact that when she became a wife, she became an instant mother. I don't care how sweet Jazmin is—motherhood is a big job to take on from day one of your marriage.

"Add that to the fact that Kelli's always been stubborn and headstrong, and it ain't no telling what's really going on. I don't care what I tried to tell her; she always went her own way. If she'd have listened to me, she'd still be teaching instead of running that store."

"The store is doing well," Wesley defended, "and I think she's doing a great job as a mother to Jazmin."

"I didn't say she wasn't doing a great job," Mary said. "Just 'cause somebody is good at a job don't mean it's a job that they enjoy."

"You don't think she likes being a mother?"

"I don't know, Wesley, but *something* is wrong. The girl ain't happy; I know that much. See, all you looking at is her outside. I know the heart of a woman. We can be smiling on the outside and crying on the inside. We can be full of life on the outside but dying on the inside. That's the way God made us. We're strong, but we're weak all at the same time."

"And you think this has something to do with Jhordan?"

"Of course it has something to do with Jhordan," Mary said. "She didn't get like this before she married him. Whether it's a problem with Jazmin or Jazmin's mother, it still stems from her involvement with Jhordan."

"Well, Mary, you saying it like she can just walk away. They're married now, and Jhordan and Tony are like the sons we never had. I like the boy. He did a good job raising that child all by himself, and I think he's an honorable man."

"I like him too, Wesley, but if he's doing something to Kelli—"

"If he's doing Kelli wrong, I'll break every bone in

his body," Wesley said. "I like him, but make no mistake—I'll kill him if I find out he's doing anything to hurt my baby girl."

Wesley reopened his paper and flipped the page to scan the local news. His eyes were fixed on the wording in front of him, but his mind was far from it. Jhordan towered over Kelli, and the heavy lifting he did on his job, coupled with his periodic visits to the local fitness center, made his strength visible to the naked eye.

Just the thought that he might be causing harm to his daughter brewed anger inside of Wesley. Though he was in reasonable shape, in a fair fight, Jhordan could beat him with no problem. But with the help of the lead pipe that he kept under his bed, Wesley believed he could be the victor.

Mary always referred to Kelli as headstrong. Most of it was due to the fact that she and their youngest daughter had done battle on several occasions during Kelli's teen years and beyond. Kelli was never disrespectful to her mother, but she definitely had a mind of her own. Thinking of it almost made Wesley laugh in spite of himself. Mary would never admit it, but the problem was that she and her daughter were so much alike.

"Maybe you're reading too much into this," Wesley said as he felt his anger dissolve. "I think Jhordan is a good man. But even more than that, I think Kelli is a smart woman. I think if she was being mistreated, she'd say so."

"Kelli ain't gonna tell us nothing," Mary said. "It would be too much like admitting I was right."

"She wouldn't tell *you*," Wesley corrected her confidently, "but she'd tell me."

"Umph," Mary grunted as she walked out of the living room and into the kitchen.

6

TEMPTATION

Thick vapors of steam encompassed Kelli as she turned off the hot water and stepped from the shower stall. After another long day at the bookstore, the refreshing shower was just what she needed. She grabbed a towel and wrapped her hair inside of it.

"Ms. Kelli," she heard Jazmin call through her bedroom door.

Kelli wrapped herself in Jhordan's thick robe and opened the door for the little girl.

"Can I get a peanut butter and jelly sandwich?" she asked.

"I'm going to fix dinner in just a minute," Kelli told her. "Why don't you grab an apple or a pear? That should tide you over for the next hour."

"Okay."

Kelli knew that the snack that the after-school program had served her must have worn off. Jazmin was a thin girl, but she loved to eat. She reminded Kelli a lot of how Cheryl was at her age. Her older sister always ate more than she did, but Kelli was the one who was always the bigger of the two.

After towel-drying her freshly shampooed hair, she tightened Jhordan's bathrobe around her body and proceeded to set the pots on the stove. Kelli's spaghetti with her father's homemade recipe for sauce was Jhordan's favorite meal for her to prepare.

She remembered her dad showing her how to combine the mixture of fresh vegetables and spices. It was about the only meal that Wesley knew how to cook, but he did it better than anyone else in the household. Kelli strained the cooked pasta and set it aside while the sauce and meat simmered together.

"Hey, Daddy!" she overheard Jazmin say as the front door opened and closed.

"Hey, pumpkin," Jhordan responded.

"Wanna play Go Fish?"

"Let Daddy get situated," he told her. "Maybe we'll play later this evening."

His answer must have placated Jazmin. Kelli heard the bedroom door close, and when she walked through the living room, Jazmin was once again content with her drawing.

"Hi," she said as she entered the bedroom.

Jhordan looked up from the mail that he was sorting through, and his eyes immediately locked on the robe that covered her body and dragged the floor beneath her feet. Still without a verbal response, she could sense his appreciation for what he saw, as his dark eyes traveled upward slowly until they met hers.

"Hi," he responded.

Kelli wanted him to walk toward her, but he seemed

cemented to the floor. Slowly dropping the envelopes to the bed, Jhordan sat on the edge but continued his gaze. Smoothing her still-damp hair behind her ears, Kelli returned his intense look. She was enthralled by what she saw. There was an invitation in the smoldering depths of his eyes.

Walking slowly toward him, Kelli came to a stop directly in front of him. With little hesitation, Jhordan reached toward her and loosened the belt that held the robe together. The touch of his hand caused her to gasp for breath. Closing her eyes, Kelli enjoyed the feel of his lips as they planted small, soft kisses from her stomach to her neck. Jhordan stood and covered her lips with his.

Kelli pulled away and pushed him back into a seated position. She straddled his lap and unloosed his shirt while kissing his face and lips.

"Oh, baby," Jhordan whispered, just before lifting her in his arms and laying her across their bed.

Kelli could feel his heart pounding as his body pressed against hers. At the base of her throat, she felt a pulse beat as though her heart had risen from its usual place. A delightful shiver of wanting ran through her, and she held him as tightly as she could.

Suddenly, as unexpectedly as it started—the sensual experience came to an end. Jhordan pulled away and stood to his feet at the side of the bed. There was still unmitigated desire in his eyes, but he backed away as he tried to gain control of his heavy breathing.

"What's wrong?" Kelli sat up and asked in concern.

"I can't do this," he muttered.

"What? Why?"

Without further explanation, Jhordan disappeared into the bathroom and locked the door behind him.

"Jhordan," Kelli called through the door. She wanted

to bang and scream, but she didn't want to startle Jazmin, who was still in the living room just beyond their closed door.

Kelli wandered back to the bed and sat. Replaying the entire intense episode in her mind, she tried to figure out what had gone wrong. On the other side of the door that separated her from her husband, she heard water streaming full speed from the bathroom faucets.

"Oh, God," she whispered as her heart pounded an erratic rhythm. "What am I doing wrong? What is going on here?"

It seemed like ages, but the running water finally subsided, and Jhordan slowly emerged. Kelli looked at him and expected an explanation of his actions. Instead, he avoided eye-to-eye contact with her and reached for the shirt she'd stripped from his body just minutes earlier.

"I'll be back," he whispered.

"You'll be back?" Kelli stared at him in amazement. "What do you mean you'll be back? You just got here."

"I'm going to take Jazmin to the movies."

"Take Jazmin to the movies?" Kelli knew she sounded like a talking parrot repeating her owner's every word, but she didn't care. "What do you mean you're taking Jazmin to the movies?"

"I mean, I'm taking her to the movies."

"Baby—" she started. Jhordan flinched when she reached for him as though he was afraid of her touch. Kelli withdrew her hand and stared at him quietly as he quickly opened the door and gave Jazmin the news.

"Yea!" she cheered.

Kelli wanted to follow him but didn't want to expose the argument to the excited girl. This wasn't Jazmin's problem, and she shouldn't be dragged into the middle of it all. Almost feeling paralyzed with disbelief, Kelli stood completely still until she heard the front door close and the car pull from the driveway.

Her first instinct was to cry, but she could find no tears. Instead, it was anger that slowly heated inside of her. The situation was worsening. Whatever or *whomever* it was that Jhordan was preoccupied with had managed to become strong enough to rip him right from her arms. On those nights that he'd sleep in the living room or not come home at all, she'd feel unattractive or, worse, rejected. This time, she experienced a sense of degradation. It was humiliating.

Picking up the telephone, she began dialing the number to her parents' house. Her father would know what to say. He always knew what to say to make her feel better. She stopped just before pressing the last number. Her mother would ultimately drag whatever she told her dad out of him. The last thing Kelli wanted to hear was an "I told you so" speech.

There was no one to talk to who would understand. She could call Sasha, but she didn't want to tarnish the fantasy image that her best friend had of Jhordan. To Sasha, Jhordan could do no wrong. And there was no way that Cheryl could understand. She and Tony had the all-American family. They actually had two kids and lived in a house surrounded by a white picket fence. A few more kids and a change of professions and they would be the Cosbys.

Grabbing her purse and reaching inside for her bottle of Advil, she fished out a crumpled piece of paper instead. Kelli didn't know why she picked the once discarded card out of the trash can at work. Opening it fully, she stared at the card. *Stuart McMillian, Attorney-at-Law.*

The temptation was too much, and her need was too great. Her hand trembled as she slowly pressed each number in the listing marked "home." Losing her nerve on the second ring, Kelli pulled the phone from her ear and prepared to hang up.

"Hello?" The voice she'd heard on only one other occasion stopped her. Still, she fought with which decision to make.

"Hello?" Stuart said again.

"Hello." Kelli spoke softly.

"May I help you?"

"Mr. McMillian?" she asked for clarification.

"Yes," he said.

"This is Kelli Adams from—"

"Racks of Reading?" he said in audible surprise.

"Yes." Kelli's tone was still soft and apprehensive.

"Well, hello," Stuart said. "You ready to talk about that divorce?"

Kelli swallowed hard, but the hot tears that she thought were lost behind her anger refused to be held back. An uncontrollable sob was the only answer she had for his sarcasm. The sound of her emotional outburst sobered him quickly.

"Kelli?" he said. "What's the matter? Are you okay? Is somebody hurting you? Where are you?" he bombarded her with one question after another.

"No."

"No, what?" Stuart's voice was almost in a panic. "No, you're not okay? No, nobody is hurting you? What?"

"I have to go." Kelli sniffled.

"Kelli," Stuart said in a warning tone, "if you hang up this phone, I swear I'll call the police and have them find you and—"

"No, don't do that," Kelli quickly said. "Please don't do that. I'm okay."

"No, you're not," he countered. "Where are you?"

"I'm at home."

"Is your husband there?"

"No. He left."

"Did he hurt you? Do you need medical help? Do you need me to call the authorities?"

"No, no, no," Kelli stopped him. "We just . . . we argued. We didn't fight—not physically. Jhordan would never hurt me. It's not like that."

"How far are you from Landry's Seafood House?" he asked after a brief silence.

"About fifteen minutes," Kelli said. "Why?"

"I'll give you twenty. If you're not there in twenty minutes, I'm going to assume you're in some kind of trouble that you're being forced not to talk about, and I'm calling the police."

"I can't meet—"

"*Twenty* minutes, Kelli." Stuart's voice was stern, and he hung up immediately after saying the words.

The traffic was heavier than normal at that hour of the night. Kelli looked at the clock on her dashboard. Just over twenty-two minutes had passed by the time she pulled into the lot of the popular seafood place along the tourist-rich street of Beach Boulevard. She could see Stuart pacing the walkway with his cell phone in hand.

She stepped from the car wearing a pair of blue jeans and a green hooded sweater. Glamorous wasn't nearly the descriptive word for her present appearance, but since getting to the assigned location before Stuart called the police was her highest priority, it was the quickest thing she could find to wear.

The coldness of the mid-December breeze against her head reminded her that she'd never finished drying her hair. She pulled the hood from her sweater over her head. After

Stuart's demand, she'd pulled it into a damp ponytail, turned off the stove, and prepared to leave. Finally noticing that it was her standing in the distant darkness, Stuart dashed across the parking lot to meet her.

"Are you all right?" he asked her while pulling her hood away and searching her head and face in the dimly lit area as though he was looking for bruises.

"I told you I was okay," Kelli said, pushing his hand away and again covering her moist hair.

"Let's go inside," he suggested.

"No."

"What? You want to stand out here in the cold?"

"No, I want to go back home," Kelli said. "I only came so you wouldn't call the police and have my face and my business all spattered across the eleven o'clock news for no good reason."

"Why are you being so difficult?" Stuart asked. "We can get a seat inside and talk about whatever it is that had you so upset less than half an hour ago."

"I don't need to talk."

"May I remind you that *you* were the one who called me?"

"My mistake."

"Kelli," Stuart said calmly. "Come on, sweetheart. Let's talk about this. I won't bite—I promise. And I'm not going to go away until I know what's going on. There are plenty of seats inside."

"They know me in there," Kelli told him. "Jhordan and I come here to eat all the time. The waitstaff knows me. I can't go in there with you."

"Fine," he sighed. Stuart leaned against her car and folded his arms. He stared straight ahead at the Christmas lights that blinked in the business across the street.

Both of them remained quiet as an approaching couple climbed into the vehicle they were standing beside and ultimately drove away. Once the coast was clear, Stuart turned and faced her. Kelli's eyes were downcast as she stared at his shoes. It was well after 8:00 p.m., and he was sharply dressed in a dark blue double-breasted suit with a grey shirt and shoes to match.

"What's really going on, Kelli?" he asked softly, giving it one last try.

"Nothing," she insisted unconvincingly.

"What did he do to you?"

She didn't answer. It was what Jhordan *didn't* do to her that had her so flustered and confused. Her brave front and hard shell were crumbling as she stood helplessly without an answer. Tears once again trembled on her eyelids. Kelli watched with watery vision as Stuart unbuttoned his coat and slowly pulled her into his chest. The comfort felt good. Yielding to the compulsive sobs, she cried freely into his chest.

7

LOVE FRUSTRATION

Jhordan watched the water roll down his front windshield as heavy drops of rainfall beat upon his truck. Three days had passed since he had walked out on Kelli, leaving her confused and vulnerable. He wanted to apologize, but her eyes were scaled with coldness and hurt every time he looked at her. He'd apologized so much to her over the past months that he knew the words hardly carried any meaning anymore.

He had everything a man could desire. With a steady job, a wife and daughter who loved him, a compassionate family, and a strong Christian faith, it seemed that he had little in his life to complain about. Yet here he was, once again, parked in an abandoned parking lot, feeling as though he was losing control of his heart, which he vowed to never fully entrust to another woman.

"I'm sorry, baby," he whispered into the darkness just as his cellular phone rang from the holster on his belt.

Though he didn't know what reason he'd give her for his extended absence, inwardly he hoped that it was Kelli. At least she'd be talking to him.

"Hello," he answered.

"Hey, Dano. How's my favorite little brother?"

Jhordan smiled. It was his sister Jeanette. Each of his sisters referred to him as their favorite brother, being that he was their only brother. However, Jeanette really was his favorite among the three of his sisters. Perhaps it was because they were barely more than a year apart in age and had grown up playing together more often than they played with their other siblings.

"Jeanette," he responded. It was good hearing from her. "To what do I owe the pleasure of this non-collect call?"

"Very funny," she said. "But let the record show that the only reason I'm not calling you collect is because you're not at home. I got your voice mail, so I thought I'd give your cell phone a try."

"Kelli wasn't home?" he asked, wondering where she could be at this hour.

"No, but I love her message on your machine. She sounds so pretty every time I speak to her. Why are you keeping her away from us? You got to bring her to Trinidad to meet the family, yes?"

"Yeah," Jhordan said. His concern slowly subsided. He was sure his wife was home—she just probably didn't answer the phone because she thought the incoming call was from him. For the first time in their marriage, he'd been introduced to the silent treatment, and he couldn't blame her.

"You're still coming in February, yes?" Jeanette asked.

"You know I can't miss Carnival," Jhordan answered. "We'll be there."

"Good," Jeanette said, "but you have more reason than Carnival to be here this time," she told him. "Although you sprung your wedding on us with too short of a notice for us to make arrangements to be there, I'm still making mine convenient for you to attend."

"Wedding?" Jhordan sat up straight. "You and Tyrique?"

"Yep!" Jeanette said with an excited laugh. "Me and Tyrique are tying the knot, and I want you and your family to be here, and I will kill you if you don't come. We're doing it during the time of the festival. Jazmin's got to be my little flower girl, and you know my favorite brother has to be here."

Tyrique Ferry was from neighboring Tobago, and he and Jeanette had been dating seriously for almost two years. He, unlike any of his other sisters' love interests, had to pass the "Jhordan test," as Jeanette called it. She'd called for her brother's assistance when Tyrique had asked her to be his steady girlfriend. Jhordan took the flight back home especially for her and met the man who had captivated his favorite sister's affections. A man of faith, ambition, and true love for his sister, Tyrique had passed the test with flying colors.

"You just want to copy me," Jhordan teased her. "I got married in February, and now you want to do the same."

"Okay, you got me." Jeanette laughed.

"We wouldn't miss it for the world, Jeanette. The two of you belong together."

"I know," she agreed. "We're going to be just like you and Kelli. She'll have to tell me all of her secrets. I want to be the perfect wife, and I want to know all that she does to make my brother happy. She's the answer to all of your prayers, yes?"

Jhordan's mind drifted at her words. Kelli, in fact, wasn't the answer to his prayers. He'd prayed for a woman he could love without losing himself. He wanted her to touch his heart, but not own it. After dating her for several months, he thought she was the answer to his prayers, but after marrying her, he found her to be more—*far* more than he'd sought God for.

Unconsciously closing his eyes, Jhordan envisioned the night he'd walked out on her. She had been so beautiful standing there in his bathrobe and even more beautiful once he'd removed it. The feel, the smell, the taste of her skin—he had been quickly engulfed by her aura.

When he had walked into the house, he could smell the aroma of the meal that he knew she was preparing just for him, but that scent had been quickly overshadowed by the fragrance of her freshly shampooed hair and her perfumed body lotion. Suddenly the hot tide of passion that raged through both of them had locked them into each other's arms.

How could he leave her like that—knowing that she wanted him so badly? How could he leave her knowing that his desires matched or exceeded her own? She was far more than he expected. His longing for her was intensified by a profound love that he didn't want to admit that he had.

"Dano?"

"Yeah?" Jhordan whispered as his eyes slowly opened.

"Something's wrong. Talk to me, little brother."

"Nothing's wrong."

"You're lying, Dano," Jeanette said. "Talk to me. Is it Kelli? She's not the sweet girl I figured her to be, no?"

"No," Jhordan quickly defended. "Kelli is the sweetest woman I've ever met. She loves me, Jeanette. I just . . ."

he said, searching for the right words. "I just don't know how—"

"How, what?" Jeanette urged. "Dano?"

"Promise me you won't tell Papa," Jhordan said. "I need this to stay between me and you. Please, Jeanette."

"Oh, no," Jeanette said. "Let me sit down. Okay, I'm sitting," she announced after a brief silence, "and I promise to keep it between the two of us. What's wrong?"

"I don't know," Jhordan said. "I married Kelli because I loved her and wanted to be with her. I thought I could be *involved* with her without falling *in love* with her."

"What?" Jeanette stopped him. "You wanted to marry her, but you weren't even in love with her?"

"Yes, I was in love with her, but I didn't think I was *this in love* with her."

"But that's a good thing, right? Isn't being *in love* with the woman you married a good thing?"

"Not for me, Jeanette."

"Dano, you're not making any sense. Why wouldn't you want to be *in love* with the woman you plan to spend the rest of your life with?"

"I've been there and done that, Jeanette. Remember? I can't put myself through that kind of misery again. When Sadonia left me, I fell completely apart. You all never saw the shell of a man I became. Papa would have disowned me if he could have seen me then. I can't do that again," he reiterated. "I need to be able to be a man about it if Kelli walks out on me. I can't do that if I'm *in love*."

"So, you don't want to fall for Kelli because of what that whore did to you?" His sister rarely ever called Sadonia by her given name. In her mind, the woman who heartlessly ripped her brother's world apart was not deserving of even the least amount of respect.

"Jeanette . . ."

"Oh, I'm sorry," she said sarcastically. "I mean *contemptible, despicable, spineless* tramp."

"She's Jazmin's mother, Jeanette."

"No," his sister corrected him. "She's no more a mother to Jazmin than are those women who people pay to have babies for them. All she did was carry her and give birth to her. *You* were Jazmin's mother until you married Kelli. Now, God has given you this magnificent wife who has become your daughter's mother, and you want to push her away because of what that poor excuse for a woman did? That's not fair, Dano."

"Fair?" Jhordan said with a pound of his fist onto the steering wheel. "Life isn't fair, Jeanette! You think it was fair what Mama did? You remember what we went through back then, all because she decided that she'd take the easy way out? You think it's fair what Sadonia did? I broke my back trying to be a good husband to her. I worked overtime to try and buy her the stuff that she wanted. I *loved* her. What did that get me, Jeanette? Huh? You think what happened to me is fair?"

"Dano, listen to yourself," Jeanette said. "Yes, Mama was selfish. Yes, your ex didn't deserve you, but Kelli shouldn't have to pay for that. You've had a lot of love frustration in your life, but you yourself just said that she loves you. That tramp that you were married to before didn't love you, and Mama—rest her soul—was too sick to realize what real love was. Again I ask, how could you marry Kelli and then not want to be *in love* with her?"

"Because I don't want to be hurt anymore, Jeanette!" Jhordan exclaimed. "I'm tired of being hurt. Both of the women I've loved with my whole heart and who had a responsibility to love me back have looked out for themselves, and what I wanted or needed didn't mean five pennies to either one of them. All I'm doing is looking out for Jhordan, for once."

"I would *hate* Tyrique if he did that to me, Dano," Jeanette said. "If Tyrique married me and then didn't want to love me the way I expected and needed to be loved, I would never be able to forgive him. If after being married to him for several months, I found out—because she *will* eventually find out—that I've been giving my whole heart to a man who doesn't want to give me his, it would kill me. Even *you'd* be angry with him, yes?"

Jhordan sat silently. He knew that if Jeanette had called and told him that, he'd be livid. His sister didn't deserve that kind of treatment, and he wouldn't tolerate her being dealt with in that manner. Jeanette had managed to back him into a corner with her comparison.

"I knew you wouldn't understand," he told her softly.

"Dano, I love you," Jeanette said. "You know I wouldn't take sides with another person if you were genuinely right. Do you want her to leave you?" she asked. "Is that what this is about? Are you looking for a way out of the marriage now that you love her more than you wanted to?"

"No," Jhordan said. "I don't *want* her to leave me. I just want to be prepared and able to handle it if she does."

"Well, prepare yourself well, little brother," Jeanette said, "because that's exactly what she's going to do. Not because she doesn't love you, but because you are going to drive her away. No woman wants to spend her life loving a man who doesn't want to love her back. And I mean *really* love her back."

"I won't let it come to that," Jhordan said. "I'll love her enough to keep her with me. If she leaves, it'll be because she's found someone else—just like Sadonia."

"No, Dano," Jeanette said. "Stop comparing the two of them. It's not the same. That piece of trash didn't *find* another man. He was in her heart all the while, and there was nothing you could have done to make her stay. On the other hand, if Kelli finds another, it'll be because the love you thought was enough really wasn't. You can't love her enough without *loving* her. There's only one kind of love that God intended for a man to have for his wife, and it's a love that can't be measured.

"That's why you're so miserable, Dano," she continued. "You have that immeasurable love for Kelli, but you're fighting it. When you fight the love that God gives you for your wife, you'll lose—and what you'll lose is *her*. You say you want to keep it so that you can be a man about it if she leaves, but how big of a man are you going to feel like, knowing that you drove the woman you truly love away?"

8

FLESH IS FLESH

S orry I'm late," Kelli said as she rushed into Racks of Reading two hours later than normal. "Jazmin wasn't feeling well this morning, so I stayed with her awhile before taking her over to my parents' house."

"Girl, you are such a good mommy," Sasha said.

"The temperature has dropped," Kelli said while pulling off her coat, "and colds are starting to go around at school. I guess she got an early one. The twins are fighting colds too, so Daddy said I might as well just bring Jazmin over and let her join them in the infirmary."

After giving Jazmin the medication that she'd bought from a neighboring drugstore, Kelli took advantage of her father's offer. She bundled her daughter in a warm jacket and delivered her to Wesley, who stood at the front door awaiting their arrival. It was obvious to Kelli that there was something that her father wanted to discuss, but to her relief, noting her haste, he hadn't pressed.

With the holidays quickly approaching, business seemed to increase on a daily basis. Sasha's abilities to run the store weren't in question, but as with most store owners, Kelli just felt more relaxed when she was on-site to ensure that everything ran smoothly. Her friend's warm personality was perfect when it came to customer service, but keeping the books in order and taking care of other business matters was Kelli's specialty. She looked out into the store and observed the stillness.

"Well, it looks pretty dead right now. When I called earlier, you told me that it was hopping in here. Did I miss the crowd?"

Sasha nodded. "Girl, there were so many people in here earlier that I've already had to replenish one of the sales tables. I'm not complaining, though. Books seem to be really big this year. There's been a steady flow of traffic all morning long. This is the first time the store's been empty since ten minutes after opening. People are definitely stocking up for Christmas. I've already had to put more children's books out on the sales table."

"Good. We'll have to check inventory and make sure we have enough to cover in the event that a last-minute rush comes through here in a couple of weeks. We don't want any angry Christmas customers," Kelli teased.

"Speaking of angry," Sasha said. "I am thoroughly prepared to tell what's-his-face off if I hear his voice on the other end of this line again today. He's called here twice for you already in the last hour and if he calls again, I'll have to pray especially hard when I hear his voice."

"Who?" Kelli asked.

"Mr. Stuart McMillian," she said.

"He's called here for me?"

"Yes," Sasha said with her hands on her hips. "Twice.

I'm trying to keep it professional, but he's just about to bring the Alabama out of me."

Kelli bit her lip. "It's okay, Sasha," she said quietly. "We had dinner the other night. He's probably just calling to follow up on our conversation. He's cool."

"You *what?*"

"It was just a friendly meal," Kelli said as she moved about, trying to keep busy so that she wouldn't have to look her friend in the face.

"A *friendly* meal? Kelli, no meal with that man is innocent. He's made it very clear that he's interested in you. Was Jhordan at this meal with the two of you?"

"No."

"Well, I know you like to be personable with your customers, but I don't think that's a good idea where Mr. McMillian is concerned. He may get the wrong idea, and he don't want to do that."

Kelli grabbed a stack of books from the credenza behind her and placed them on the counter.

"He won't get the wrong idea," she responded.

Still unconvinced, Sasha continued. "Girl, if Jhordan finds out that that man is sweet on you, he'll—"

"He'll what, Sasha?" Kelli snapped as she turned to face her. "What is Jhordan gonna do, huh? Is he going to go into a jealous rage? Is he going to confront him and fight for me?"

"Why are you saying it like he won't?" Sasha said. "If Stuart McMillian touches you—"

"Then it'll be the first time I've been touched in weeks!" Kelli cut into her sentence again.

"What?"

"He doesn't touch me, Sasha," Kelli said as she held back tears of frustration. "Jhordan won't touch me, and every time I try to get close to him, he pushes me away."

Caught off guard, Sasha stood speechless and watched as Kelli, at record pace, typed the ISBN numbers into the computer to register the books in their catalog. Very few times had Kelli ever known her talkative friend to be without words, but for several moments staring seemed to be the only form of communication she could muster.

"Are we talking about *my* Jhordan?" she asked when she finally found her voice.

"Yes, Sasha," Kelli assured her. "We're talking about that Jhordan!"

"Are you telling me that he's *impotent?*" Sasha whispered as though the word were profane.

"No. If that was the problem, I could understand. It's not that he *can't* be with me—he *won't* be with me. I know he's capable. Believe me, he's *highly* competent."

"Then what's the problem?"

"I don't know, Sasha; I guess it's me. I don't think he wants to be with me." Kelli whisked a lone tear from her cheek. "I keep trying not to think that there's another woman, but what else could there be?"

"Kelli!"

"No, Sasha, listen. Last week, he walked out *while* we were . . . you know."

"You mean he walked out on you right in the middle of it?"

"Not in the middle of it," Kelli explained. "It was more like the onset of it. But the stage was set, the lights were on, the curtains were opening, and all systems were go, and he just stopped and walked out. Maybe he had a date with *her* and didn't want to mess it up by being with me."

"No, Kelli. I just can't believe that Jhordan would do that to you."

"We've only been married less than a year, Sasha, and the magic left before it had a chance to get started. I don't know what's wrong with me." More tears spilled from her eyes as her voice broke.

"I'm sorry, Kelli," Sasha said with a warm embrace. "I didn't know. How come you didn't tell me?"

"What woman wants to announce that her husband doesn't find her attractive, Sasha? I was hoping it would go away, but instead it's getting worse. Is this what I saved myself for?" Kelli asked, wiping her tears with the tissue that her friend offered.

"I waited until I was twenty-eight years old to get married when all of the girls I knew were getting married at twenty-two and twenty-three. I thought I was doing everything right. I got my education and got my professional life together before I even began considering seriously dating a man. When I got to the point that I wanted to be married, I prayed so hard for the right man to come along.

"I asked God for a man who would love me so much. I wanted a man whose love for me would match my love for him. I *love* Jhordan, Sasha—I love him so much, but I don't think he loves me, and I'm starting to feel like a fool for sticking around."

"Physical satisfaction and desire isn't the determining factor of whether or not someone loves you, Kelli. You know that."

"He's my husband, Sasha. He's supposed to love me in *every* way."

"So what are you saying?" Sasha challenged. "Are you telling me that because Jhordan isn't fulfilling his physical duties to you as a husband, you're turning to another man?"

"Of course not! Stuart has a good ear, and he listens

to me—that's all it is. I needed someone to talk to, and he was there for me."

"He's a divorce lawyer, Kelli," Sasha said. "He's paid to listen to dissatisfied married men and women on a daily basis. And not only is he a divorce lawyer, but he's a divorce lawyer who is attracted to you. The combination of that and the fact that you are very vulnerable spells trouble. It's a trap—I can't believe that you don't see it!"

"I'm not naïve, Sasha. I'm in this with my eyes wide open. I'm not going to him for surrogate affection. I know he's accustomed to listening to people's troubles; that's why he's good for me. I need someone who will listen right now. Stuart has been a godsend for me over the past few days."

Sasha was shocked at her friend's thinking. Kelli had always been the smart one. In school—even in the company—she was the one with all the good business sense and the know-how to handle even the most difficult situations. It was as if some other being had taken over her mind and had convinced her to trust a man that Sasha knew wasn't worthy of the confidence Kelli was placing in him.

"Sasha," Kelli spoke, noting the disturbed look on her face. "God knew I needed somebody to listen to me without being judgmental, and He sent the most unlikely person my way. Stuart has been nothing but supportive. He hasn't tried to make Jhordan out to be a monster, and he hasn't made any inappropriate moves on me."

"Yet," Sasha said.

"Sasha—"

"Now, I know I'm not all deep in the Scriptures, and I don't go to church every Sunday like you do," Sasha said, "but even I can see that this is a trap."

"Face it, Sasha. You've never liked him from the moment he came in here. You're not even giving him a fair chance."

"True," Sasha admitted, "but this really isn't about my personal feelings about the man. This is about my concern for you. I don't know what Jhordan's problem is, and I ain't saying that he's right for what he's putting you through. But I do know that Stuart McMillian is not the one for you to confide in.

"You are two attractive, professional adults, Kelli. He finds you appealing, and you and I both know he's fine. It don't matter how many times a day you pray or how many times a week you go to church—flesh is flesh."

Before Kelli could respond, the front door opened, and a new stream of customers began coming in, bringing the conversation to a premature end. Kelli brushed the lingering tears away and put on her best business face. Stuart was right. No one who was close to her and Jhordan as a couple would understand, because on the outside people perceived the Adams, as the "perfect couple."

Sasha had reacted just the way Stuart had predicted. So what if he'd openly flirted with her upon their first meeting? He'd now proven that the first impression shouldn't always be the lasting one. He knew her level of commitment to her marriage, and he was there to help her save it. He was the friend that God had provided in her time of need. Kelli wished Sasha could see that, but she couldn't spend her time worrying that she refused to.

9

THE UPPER ROOM

S ome things in life never seemed to change. Summer would always follow spring, winter would always follow fall, and no matter what the season, Sunday
afternoons would always mean a table full of food and
unending conversation at the Jenkins' home.

Good table manners weren't demanded or even expected. Somebody's elbows were always on the table,
mouths that were full of food didn't stop talking, and
teeth-picking wasn't a rarity. Nobody tried to be proper—
it was just family. It was an improper yet endearing tradition that had been handed down from generation to
generation. Kelli's family could've starred in *Soul Food*.

"Mama," Tony said as he licked the creamy sauce
off of his fork, "you put your foot in this macaroni and
cheese today."

"Thank you, honey." Mary beamed.

Another Sunday morning had come and gone. The

church service had been enjoyable, and since it was a Sunday that Jhordan had to work all day, Kelli decided that it was a good day for her and Jazmin to eat dinner with her family. As the family grew, Wesley didn't bother to purchase another kitchen table; he'd just squeeze another chair in at the one that they'd had since his daughters were small.

Tony was right. Mary Jenkins had always been labeled as the best at cooking Southern food, but today's secret blend of five cheeses in her macaroni casserole was exceptional. As delicious as it was, though, Kelli could only bring herself to eat a little of the dinner that her mom had put so much work into.

"Watching your weight, Kelli?" Wesley said upon noticing her still-almost-full plate.

"Umph!" Mary grunted. "You got your mama's hips, girl. Ain't no sense in trying to lose 'em. Those are child-bearing hips. You gonna need 'em, so you better feed 'em."

"I'm not watching my weight," Kelli said over the laughter that ran around the table. "I guess I'm just not all that hungry today."

"Are you feeling okay?" Cheryl asked in motherly concern.

"You should have let Pastor Berry pray for you," Mary said. "Talk about a man who can get a prayer through! Oooh, child! The anointing just be all over that man. He can pray for me anytime. I don't know why you didn't marry him when you had a chance."

"Mama!" Kelli scolded, throwing a glance in Jazmin's direction as she spoke.

"Are you sick, Kelli?" her father asked, interrupting what promised to be an unpleasant exchange between the women.

"No," Kelli said. "I feel fine. Really. I ate kind of late last night, and I guess I just don't have the appetite that I usually have on Sundays."

"Last night?" Tony scowled. "I don't care how late I may have eaten last night. That was then, and this is now. It's 3:00 in the afternoon, sis-in-law. Whatever you ate last night is long gone by now."

"What did you cook last night?" Wesley asked.

Mary began looking troubled as she got up and walked around the table to feel Kelli's forehead for signs of a temperature.

"Probably ate some junk food, didn't you?" she asked. "You just like your daddy. You can be sick as a dog and won't tell a soul."

"I feel fine, Mama," Kelli assured her.

"What did you cook?" Mary echoed her husband's earlier inquiry.

"I didn't cook, Mama. I went out and got something to eat. I'm not sick. I'm fine."

The fuss they were making over her unwillingness to stuff her face with the three-course meal that still sat in front of her was getting to be too much. Kelli picked up her fork and began picking through her beef stew.

"So, you and Jhordan took advantage of the fact that Jazmin was spending the night with us, and y'all decided to go on a date, huh?" her father said, sporting a wide grin of approval. "It's good to get out like that every once in a while."

"I thought Jhordan was pulling a double shift," Tony added. "He was working last night, wasn't he?"

"Yes," Kelli said, hoping that the conversation would soon end. "I didn't go out with Jhordan. I drove my own car and went out to get a bite to eat. I guess I overate, because I'm not really hungry right now."

"Where'd you go?" Cheryl asked.

"Can we talk about something else?" Kelli pleaded after looking into Jazmin's inquisitive eyes as she sat beside her, quietly eating the last of her food.

"Why?" Mary's eyes were narrowed with suspicion.

"Because it's irrelevant where I ate, Mama," Kelli said. "Is it a crime that I'm not hungry today?"

"Jazmin," Mary said without taking her eyes off of Kelli. "Take your plate and go in the playroom and finish eating at the table in there."

"Mama . . ." Kelli started. Her mother's eyes were set with a look of warning, and against her better judgment, Kelli conceded. "Go ahead, sweetie," she told her stepdaughter.

"Here," Cheryl said as she pulled the twins from their high chairs and placed them onto the floor. "You can take Tonya and Christopher with you if you'd like."

"Okay. I'm done eating anyway," Jazmin concluded as she led the toddlers away.

No one spoke until the children had cleared the dining area and the closing of the door to the playroom down the hall had been heard. Even then, there was momentary silence, but Mary ended it quickly.

"Spill it."

"Mama, why did you do that?" Kelli asked.

"No, no, no," Mary said while waving her hand out in front of her and shaking her head. "Don't try to change the subject. What is it that you're not telling us?"

"Why are you making such a big deal out of this?" Kelli asked. "There's nothing to tell you. Do I have to share every detail of how I spent my day?"

"I tell you what," Mary said as she stood back with one hand perched on her hip. "I don't know what you hiding, but it's high time you start making it clear. Now

I suggest that whatever it is you did, you gone on ahead and tell us and don't make us try to guess at it. From where I stand, all the secrecy ain't making it sound too good. Now what is it?"

Mary had taken on that look that she'd give them as children when she was extending to them one last chance to tell the truth about something before she went to their father's drawer and pulled out one of his long leather belts. Kelli knew that Mary Jenkins wasn't going to let it go easily.

"Will everybody just calm down?" Kelli asked with a deep sigh. "I didn't go and commit an armed robbery or anything. You all act as though you think I went and took something from somebody."

"We ain't worried about whether or not you took nothing *from* nobody," Mary said as she returned to her seat. "We worried about whether or not you *gave* something to somebody."

"Mama!" Kelli exclaimed, immediately realizing what her mother was insinuating. "Is that what you all think of me?" she asked.

"Okay, that's enough," her father said.

Mary ignored her husband and continued. "Your husband was at work, Kelli," she said while settling back in her seat. "I know you ain't been all that happy lately. You ain't said nothing, but you can't pull the wool over my eyes. I knew from the beginning there was gonna be trouble, and I tried to tell you, but you wouldn't listen."

"Mary," Wesley warned.

"You didn't go out by yourself," she continued, "and I know you're hiding something. I don't know what it is or who *he* is, but like I said, all this secrecy ain't making it look good."

"I went out with a friend, okay?" Kelli blurted angrily.

"It was a simple dinner at a simple restaurant. That's all it was! There were no illicit acts being carried out, Mama. It was a nice evening, and I am *so very sorry* if I disappointed you by being a respectable lady and not doing the horizontal mambo with every man I have a casual dinner with!"

Kelli folded her arms and fought tears as the dining room came to a complete hush. Mary had always spoken her mind for as long as Kelli could remember. She never bit her tongue for anybody, and no one ever really knew what she might let out of her mouth. Wesley, however, was a different story. He always kept a level head, and it took a lot to ruffle his feathers. Raising his voice was a rarity, but when he did, he got everyone's undivided attention. A dropped pin could have been heard after he called for order at the table.

"Now apologize to your mama." His voice had returned to its normal level but remained stern as he looked toward his youngest daughter.

"I'm sorry," Kelli whispered with her eyes fixed on the tablecloth.

"Now everybody finish eating your food," Wesley ordered with a toss of his napkin onto the table. "And you," he turned to Kelli, "come with me."

In obedience, Kelli slowly got up from the table and followed her father. He led the way out of the dining room and up the stairs so that they'd be away from everyone's listening range. Flashbacks in her head made Kelli all of a sudden feel thirteen years old again.

It was the place where they'd go as a family and pray when she was younger. The handmade sign that she and Cheryl had designed eighteen years ago had somewhat faded, but it was still held to the wall with the same thumbtacks they'd used back then. In every color in the paint kit, the sign said The Upper Room, affectionately named after the place in the Bible where Christ had His disciples meet for prayer following His resurrection.

Kelli finally broke the silence. "I'm sorry, Daddy. I didn't intend to yell. I guess I just . . . I'm sorry," she repeated.

"You know, every time I look at you," Wesley started, "I see your mama. Cheryl is mostly like me. You, on the other hand—you're just like Mary. You got her looks, you got her build, and you even got her ways. She might not be right all the time, Kelli, but she's still your mama, and even though you grown and married, you need to remember that."

"I've never raised my voice to Mama before," Kelli said. "It just made me so angry when she basically accused me of sleeping with another man. That really hurt."

"I know," her father said. He leaned forward and propped his elbows on his knees and sat face-to-face with her. "Tell me about this man."

"Do you think I'd be unfaithful to Jhordan, Daddy?"

"Of course not, baby," he said. "I know we raised you well, and I know you love your husband."

"But Mama thinks so, doesn't she? How could she think I'd do that?"

"Let me tell you something that you don't know," her father began.

He pulled her close to him as he spoke as though she were a little child. For as long as Kelli could recall, it had always been easier to talk to her dad. Unlike Cheryl and most other girls she knew growing up, when there was a subject matter that she wanted to talk about—especially one of a sensitive nature—she would be more comfortable going to her father. She couldn't exactly verbalize why he was her parent of choice, but to Kelli, Wesley seemed more understanding and patient with her. She knew that her mother loved her just as much as he, but she'd always seemed to draw conclusions before hearing the full story. Wesley Jenkins was just a better listener.

When Kelli and Cheryl were children, Wesley worked long hours—taking odd jobs after his bus route was complete—and didn't get to spend as much time with his growing girls as his wife did. Perhaps that made the time that he did spend with them more meaningful, and he didn't want to use that time being such a harsh disciplinarian. He tightened the reins when they got out of line, but his nature was more gentle, and even though he was rarely home when they got in from school, Kelli would hold whatever it was that she needed to talk about until he was there to listen.

"When you and Cheryl were little girls," he said, "me and your mama prayed real hard for both of you. It may be a silly and unfounded thing, but when you got girls, it just seems like a whole lot more responsibility than boys. You'll find out as Jazmin gets older.

"When Mary was pregnant with you," he continued, "you kicked harder and moved way more often than your sister did. There were many nights when your mama couldn't get much sleep because of your activity inside her belly. We joked way back then that you were gonna be a challenge."

"I don't think I like what that suggests," Kelli defended.

"Turns out," Wesley said, "it wasn't a bad thing at all. You've always been determined, and you've always been a fighter. You were walking before you learned to crawl good. You started talking early, you were potty trained in a week's time, and it just never seemed like you were a baby. When you wanted to be spoiled, you always came to me. I'm not complaining, because I enjoyed every minute of it. But I don't think your mama ever felt like you needed her.

"She won't ever admit it, but I know that it's because of that, that she can be very overbearing when it comes to you. She's still trying to be the mother that you seemed to outgrow so early in life. She don't mean no harm, Kelli. You have to know that."

"No harm?" Kelli said in disbelief. "Daddy, do you know what Mama was just accusing me of? How could she think I'd go there? She should know me better than that. How could suggesting something like that not harm me?"

"Baby, charge it to her head and not her heart," Wesley said as he pulled her even closer to him. "Just like she should know you better—you should know her by now too. Your mama knows you ain't been out there doing that kind of stuff. That's just her way of trying to find out exactly what's going on in your life. I ain't saying it's right. I'm just saying that it's just your mama's way. She knows how much you love Jhordan too."

"Well, she didn't have to send Jazmin out of the room," Kelli said. "She's a smart girl. She knows something was wrong. Now I'm going to have to explain everything to her on the ride home. I'm twenty-nine years old, Daddy, and I have a family of my own. Mama took it too far."

"You're absolutely right"—Wesley nodded—"but I promise you—it was only out of genuine concern. Are you telling me that you can't see that? If your mama didn't react that way, she wouldn't be your mama. You know that all she wants is the best for you."

"I guess." Kelli shrugged. "But I think she owes me an apology too. You made me apologize to her, but you didn't make her apologize to me."

"That's why I been a happily married man for almost forty years." Wesley smiled. "Your mother just needs a little time to let herself cool off, and she'll do what's right. I ain't 'bout to embarrass her by making her say she's sorry to her child. She'll do it on her own when she's ready."

Kelli smiled and accepted the hug that her father offered.

"I'm really sorry, Daddy."

"We're not done," he said as he released her.

"I know."

"Tell me what you're going through that you can't talk to your husband about. Who is this man you had dinner with?"

In spite of the fact that she still felt that her business with Stuart was still *her* business, Kelli was relieved to be able to talk to someone about it who would listen.

"His name is Stuart McMillian. He's an attorney with McMillian At Law, and he's a customer at the bookstore. I just needed somebody to talk to, Daddy, and I couldn't talk to Jhordan."

"Why couldn't you come to me or your mother?"

"Daddy, you know how skeptical Mama was about me marrying Jhordan in the first place. I wasn't in any mood to hear *the speech* from her. You heard her just then. She's all cranked up to remind me of what she said back then."

"Does this have to do with Jhordan's ex-wife? Are you having problems?"

"No. I still haven't spoken to her—which is fine by me. Last night, she and Jhordan had an argument about something, but I didn't ask what it was concerning, and he didn't voluntarily tell me. I've never had to deal with her personally."

"What is it then?" Wesley probed. "Is he mistreating you?"

"Jhordan is very gentle, Daddy. He's not physically abusing me, if that's what you're asking." Kelli put his worst fears to rest.

"Is *he* being unfaithful? Is that what you don't want us to know?"

Kelli looked at him in silence. The possibility of it placed sourness in the pit of her stomach. Closing her eyes briefly, she tried to erase the images of Jhordan passionately embracing another woman.

"Oh, child," Wesley whispered while brushing his hand across his forehead.

"I don't know, Daddy," she quickly spoke up. "I don't know that he's seeing someone else, I just know that he and I aren't . . ." She sighed and began again. "We've only been together a few times since we've been married, and I know that he's purposely avoiding me. Maybe it's not that he wants someone else. Maybe it's just that he *doesn't* want me."

"That's nonsense," Wesley said as he stood and paced the floor with his hands shoved in his pockets.

"I started to call the firehouse last night just to see if he was really pulling a double shift, but I didn't. I don't think I wanted to know the truth. As long as I didn't know that he *wasn't* there, then I could pretend that he was."

"You have to talk with him, Kelli," her father said. "Now, not only is he avoiding you, but you're avoiding him, and both of you are avoiding the issues. A marriage can't survive like that. If you don't have trust and communication, you don't have anything."

"That's what Stuart said."

"Well, I could be wrong," Wesley said as he sat in

front of her once more, "but I'd almost bet you anything that I'm giving you entirely different advice than your lawyer friend is. I'm saying that the two of you need to close the gap that has grown between you. Stuart, on the other hand, is probably hinting that if you can't trust or communicate with Jhordan, then there's no need of you staying in the marriage."

"I don't think so, Daddy."

"All I'm saying is that you need to watch yourself. Going behind Jhordan's back and having secret meetings with this man is no better than whatever it is that Jhordan is doing and not disclosing to you. You're a grown woman now, Kelli. I wish I could make your decisions for you, but I can't. My advice is for you to cut ties with Mr. McMillian and work on your marriage. If you take a step back and look at the situation, I'm sure you'll agree.

"If you need me, you know I'm here. But unless you ask for my intervention, I'm going to stay out of it and allow you and your husband to work out your differences. I want your marriage to survive. If he's being unfaithful, he has totally managed to pull the wool over my eyes, and that's not easy to do. I believe that God put the two of you together and gave that precious little girl in there the family that she deserves. Don't let evil come in and destroy what God has done."

"You think Stuart is evil?"

"Honestly?"

"Yes."

"Yes," Wesley said. "If I didn't love you, I'd tell you what you wanted to hear, but since I do, I have to tell you what you *need* to hear. I don't know the man, but I know his type. And more importantly, I know that God will not send a member of the opposite sex to console you at a time like this. You're a smart girl, Kelli —watch yourself."

Kelli couldn't believe that the one person who'd always understood her didn't share the same view of Stuart. She still didn't agree, but Kelli was tired of trying to convince everyone of Stuart's sincerity. Everybody doubted his intentions. Stuart had warned her, but she was so sure that her father, of all people, would be more open-minded and not so quick to judge a man that he didn't even know. In spite of everything, Kelli knew that her father's advice was given out of a heart that meant well.

"Thanks, Daddy." Kelli hugged him again.

"Now you know we can't leave without praying together."

"It wouldn't be the Upper Room if we didn't." Kelli smiled.

Following the prayer that Wesley led while holding his daughter's hands, the two came out of the room and made their way back to the ground floor of the split-level house. Dinner was over and the house was quiet. Tony and Cheryl sat snuggled together on the couch watching television while Jazmin patiently taught the twins how to properly stack blocks so that they wouldn't fall so easily. As her father walked toward his bedroom, Kelli walked toward the sound of pots and pans being put away.

Mary closed the cabinet after putting the last dish away and turned to face her youngest daughter. She laid the dish towel on the counter and silently walked toward Kelli. Neither of them spoke a word. A long, heartfelt embrace shared between them was all the communication that was needed.

10

A HERO AIN'T NOTHIN' BUT A SANDWICH

It had been a very busy day to end another extremely long week. Between a full workload that included capping the teeth of a woman preparing to run for the next Miss New York beauty pageant and the three hours she'd spent shopping on 47th Street, Sadonia Burton was tired. Now in her eighth year as an oral surgeon in a top-notch New York dental practice, she'd brushed shoulders with everyone from politicians to Oscar-winning movie stars.

Every Friday she treated herself for the hard work that earned her the big check. Sometimes it was a hairdo. Other times she'd enjoy a total body pampering at a local five-star spa. Today it was a formal, four-piece interchangeable outfit that was sure to catch the eyes of some very fine men—both single and married—at the annual Christmas gathering that was now just over a week away.

With a full glass of wine in one hand, she walked to

her telephone and listened to each of the eight messages that were waiting. Disappointed at what she heard—or *didn't* hear—she took a long sip before heading into her master bathroom where tension-releasing hot water awaited.

"Men!" she exclaimed with a grimace before setting her glass on the side of the porcelain heart-shaped bathtub and slipping out of her clothes.

Sadonia had just about had her fill of the fast-paced, overrated New York dating scene. Recent relationships hadn't been fulfilling for her. It had been a week since she'd had Dr. Ralph Emory over for an intimate evening for two. The specialist served on the staff of gynecology practitioners at the popular Mount Sinai Hospital on 5th Avenue.

She'd gone in for a routine yearly checkup and had met him when they were both leaving the building. He'd said that he was immediately attracted to her overall beauty, but it was her intelligence that captivated him the most.

Ralph really wasn't her type at all. Sadonia liked her men tall, dark, and handsome. At six feet two, Ralph scored one out of three. By far, he didn't qualify for her list of best-looking dates, and with his curly blond hair and ocean-blue eyes, he was a far cry from dark. It was the status of dating a physician like herself that finally convinced Sadonia to accompany him for an evening out on the town.

He'd left her house at nearly 3:00 last Sunday morning after he'd hounded her for weeks for a chance to take her out, and she hadn't heard a word from him since he kissed her goodnight.

In two big gulps, Sadonia finished off the red wine and looked at her teary-eyed reflection in the mirror. By now, it seemed as though she would have learned her lesson about men and money. Pete Burton should have been all the learning experience that she needed. Marrying a man with money may have secured her lifestyle, but she was proof positive it was no guarantee for happiness.

She'd been romanced by several men in her life—if you could call it romance. Being with them only satisfied temporary physical needs, but none of them genuinely loved her. None, but—

"Oh, Jhordan," she whispered. "If I could do it all over again . . ."

The thought of her own misguided stupidity made angry tears roll down her cheek. Quickly stepping into the tub, she sat and relaxed against her bath pillow and allowed the silent tears to flow freely from her closed eyes.

Jhordan was the only man to love her the way she needed and wanted to be loved, and she threw it all away for a man with seemingly unlimited funds who promised her heaven, but instead gave her a one-way ticket to her own private hell.

She'd wished a million times over the past five years that she could take it all back and reclaim her first husband's affections, but anything that she'd tried was too little too late. Jhordan had begged her not to leave him. Instead of his tears softening her heart, she'd called him a sorry excuse for a man and told him to get a *real* job, and then perhaps he'd deserve a *real* woman.

She'd given up everything to marry the man who'd once been her high school sweetheart and had returned to New York as a high-powered, much-respected business tycoon. Next to Pete, Jhordan and his job with the New York Fire Department seemed trivial. The fact that firefighters and police officers were viewed as heroes by most of the rest of the world meant nothing to her.

Jhordan had actively risked his life to save people he didn't know in the fires that followed the attack on the World Trade Center on that fateful day now dubbed simply "9/11." Still, for Sadonia, it was the money that spoke the loudest, and she had no desire to return to the man she'd left.

"A hero ain't nothin' but a sandwich," she'd said in a mocking tone in reference to Jhordan's job when a friend asked how she could see Pete's sometimes cutthroat profession as a better one than Jhordan's career, which involved saving lives. "And a sandwich can't buy me these," Sadonia had concluded while touching the diamond earrings that dangled from her ears.

Now she'd give almost anything for another taste of that "sandwich," but she realized that what she'd done to both Jhordan and Jazmin was unforgivable. In addition, Sadonia knew that if she were in his shoes, she wouldn't even be as kind as he'd been. For the past three summers, he'd allowed her to keep the daughter that she'd totally signed over to him. Even after the way she'd treated him, Jhordan had allowed Sadonia to continue a relationship with their daughter, though it wasn't easy for Jhordan. He'd become selfless and forgiving enough to permit it. It was clear to Sadonia that he didn't "play church" like she did; he truly had a real relationship with the Lord.

In her heart of hearts, she still loved him, and it distressed her to know that she'd never have the opportunity to be with him again. He'd made that unmistakably clear. It had been the root of the argument that she'd had with him by telephone last Saturday. She'd used a desire to see Jazmin as the reason for her call, but in reality it was a desire to see Jhordan that had motivated her to pick up the phone. He'd picked up on her obvious ploy.

She'd been particularly lonely that day and longed for the touches to her body that only Jhordan had mastered. He'd loved her once—maybe there was still a trace in his heart of what he once felt for her. She knew it was a long shot, but the worst he could say was no.

"Sadonia," he'd said in a tone laced with fury, "I'm trying with everything in me to have true forgiveness for you, but even in forgiveness I will never trust, love, or have a morsel of desire for you again. I'd rather die a slow, agonizing death and have my flesh eaten by wild beasts than to lie with you."

The words had cut and burned as though an old, rusty pocketknife laced in alcohol had been used to slice into her chest. She couldn't have felt any more rejected and worthless had he thrown dirt in her face. They argued, but only briefly before Jhordan disconnected the call. She knew she deserved it, but that didn't ease the pain. It was that event that led her to call Ralph and succumb to the meaningless, regretful night they'd spent together.

"Oh, God," she whispered.

Her life had long ago taken a downward spiral. Though she'd climbed the corporate ladder and was now making the money and living at the standard that she'd been aiming for, she had fallen a long way down from the place where her spiritual life had once been. When she first met and married Jhordan, she was at least trying to be the woman and the wife that she knew God wanted her to be.

"If Pete had never come back here . . ." she began. "No!" she scolded, stopping herself.

Ever since she'd decided to leave Jhordan for grass she had thought was greener, Sadonia had been blaming one person or another for the stupid decisions that she'd made.

Pete and his return to New York had been her point of blame for the reason she'd left the church, Jhordan, and her daughter. Jhordan's rejection of her attempts to reconcile, following Pete's departure, had been the blame for the buffet of men she'd dined with and on since her second failed marriage. Kelli, the woman Jazmin couldn't stop talking about, had been the blame for why Jhordan wouldn't give her the one last chance she requested.

Too poor to get the things she wanted growing up, Sadonia felt she *deserved* the "finer things" in life, no matter what the cost. But in a heartbeat, she knew that she'd relinquish all the money to once again be the wife of a common fireman. Her affair with Pete had only been the beginning of the heartbreak that she'd caused Jhordan. The damage was irreversible, and she was amazed at how he'd been able to put the shattered pieces of his life back together and share his full self with a new woman.

Despite her envy toward Kelli for having what she could only wish for, Sadonia found a strange sense of comfort that Jhordan had once again found love and been strong enough to trust another woman with his heart.

"You deserve to be happy," Sadonia whispered as she wiped lingering tears of regret.

Her thoughts were genuine. She really did want the best for him, but in all truthfulness, she wanted him to find that happiness with her. Sadonia wondered within herself if Jhordan was truly happy with his new wife and how she could find out. If there was even a smidgen of a chance that beneath the animosity he had for her there was any love left—any at all . . .

11

A CHANGE IS
GONNA COME

Stuart sat at a table for two located perfectly in an almost secluded corner of Bayside Restaurant. The popular eatery, as usual for a Saturday evening, was filled almost to capacity. From where he sat, he had a clear view of the bar. Even that area, which was normally not as busy, seemed to overflow with people who didn't come in early enough to get a table on the floor.

His mind raced as he sipped his second glass of ginger ale and glanced at his Rolex. Kelli was late. Could he have assumed wrong? Did her husband actually decide to stay at home tonight instead of disappearing as normal, leaving her wondering what or *who* he was doing?

Stuart had already been there for half an hour. He wanted to be sure to beat the rush and to get the corner table. The McMillian name came in useful on nights like this. Bayside was a regular eating spot for them when they treated their favorite clients to lunch. A simple call guaranteed him the prime spot where he could talk to Kelli alone.

The waitress returned to his table and filled his glass for the third time. The stress of not knowing if or when Kelli would arrive was beginning to dry out his mouth and throat. The moisture from the soft drink was refreshing, but if she didn't show up, he'd need a martini to drown his disappointment.

"I get off in an hour," his waitress said, flirting. "If she doesn't show, you can wait around for something better."

Her name was Lynda, and Stuart knew her well. She was blonde and busty, and it was that kind of flirting that got her into his Mercedes a couple of months ago. Lynda was young—twenty-one or twenty-two, maybe—too young for Stuart to have any real interest in. She aimed to please, though, and that was all he needed from a woman.

"If she doesn't show," he said, "we'll talk."

"I'll keep my fingers crossed," she said with a smile.

Stuart smiled back and gave her a quick wink. Tonight his interests were elsewhere. He'd put a lot of time and effort into building a trusting relationship with Kelli, and he almost had her where he wanted her. Women like Lynda weren't hard to get. If he didn't take her home tonight, he knew she'd still be available and willing the next time he came.

"I suggest you keep your fingers crossed too," she added.

The sight of Kelli entering the restaurant served as a plug for Stuart's ears. Though Lynda continued to talk, he unintentionally tuned out her voice and the other chatter in the restaurant. All he could hear was Barry White's voice singing "You Turn My Whole World Around" as his dinner date seemed to walk in slow motion, toward his table. She wore an eye-catching jade-colored silk pantsuit that flowingly flattered her every curve.

Finally realizing that she was being ignored, Lynda muttered and stepped aside to give the couple more space as Stuart pulled Kelli's chair out from the table. At the same time, he realized that the song he was hearing wasn't just ringing in his ears. It was coming over the speaker system in the restaurant.

"Can I bring you something to drink?" the disappointed waitress asked.

"Sweet tea would be fine," Kelli said.

"You look very nice," Stuart complimented once he was seated.

"Thank you," she said, trying to shake the echoing of her father's warning from her ears.

"I guess your being here means Jhordan disappeared again." He tried hard and succeeded in masking the feelings of elation and victory that he felt as he spoke.

Kelli turned away and stared into the distance at nothing in particular. This time Jhordon had left while she was showering. He hadn't even said good-bye. She'd stepped from the shower and found a note from him that he'd return shortly. That was at 7:00 p.m. When she left the house at 8:15, he still hadn't returned.

With Jazmin spending the night at Cheryl and Tony's, Kelli hoped that it would be an opportunity for her and her husband to have some time alone to discuss whatever it was that was driving them further and further apart. Her hopes weren't even given a chance to become reality.

"I'm sorry, sweetheart," Stuart said after the silence continued. "I really am," he lied. Reaching across the table, he placed his hand on top of hers and patted it in bogus support.

"I don't know what to do," Kelli said softly. "I'm all out of ideas."

Stuart saw signs of tears in her eyes. He sort of felt sorry for her—but he needed to stay focused on his *own agenda*.

That agenda involved Stuart getting Kelli to a place where her heart was hardened against Jhordan. He wanted her to be at a place where whether Jhordan was doing all the right things or not, she couldn't care less.

Lynda returned with Kelli's drink and remained at the table long enough to take their orders. Before walking away, she stopped behind Kelli's back and gave Stuart a look to let him know that she wasn't exactly thrilled that he seemed so into the woman who shared his table.

"Don't give up yet, Kelli," Stuart told her, ignoring Lynda's silent message. "The male species can be difficult sometimes. I know because I've been one of them for thirty-three years."

Kelli slipped her hand from under his and picked up her drink so it didn't seem that she was consciously pulling away from him.

"That's no excuse," she said. "Females are far more complex than males. Compared to us, you all are pretty shallow, actually. Besides," she continued, "I could understand difficult. All of us have our days, but Jhordan is being way beyond difficult. I've never felt like this before—it's so hard to describe how his actions make me feel."

Their food finally arrived, but Lynda wasn't the one to bring it to them. Shortly before the waiter brought their meals to them Stuart briefly locked eyes with Lynda as she was gathering her things together to leave. Her shift had ended, and from her demeanor, it was obvious that she'd hoped that his dinner date had gone sour and she'd be accompanying him home once again.

He had bigger fish to fry, and the fire was already lit under the pan. Kelli was a different kind of girl, though. He couldn't approach her with the same forwardness as he'd done with Lynda a few weeks ago. The flame under the frying pan had to be increased slowly. She would never have given him a second of her time if he'd handled her as he'd handled Lynda. It would take him longer to collect the reward for his troubles, but he was a patient man when he wanted to be. And when the prize was as beautiful as Kelli, he had all the patience in the world. He knew it was only a matter of time.

"So where do you go from here?" he asked as they began enjoying their meals.

"I don't know," Kelli answered. "All I can do is keep hoping and praying. I have to believe that a change is gonna come, or else I don't know what other choices I have."

"Kelli—" Stuart started.

"I know what you're going to say," Kelli said, stopping him. "You're going to tell me not to make any quick decisions. I've heard you all one hundred times you've said it before," she said. "I'm trying to be patient, Stuart. I really am."

"Trying is all you can do," Stuart responded.

It was all he needed to hear. To know that she was contemplating leaving Jhordan was enough to get his mind racing. It meant that everything was happening right on target. All he'd need is one more week, maybe two, to solidify his plan.

There were ideas in his mind that he hadn't even discussed with her yet, like how to move on without the husband who had apparently found a way to move on without her. But now wasn't the time to discuss it. He couldn't get ahead of himself. The wheels were already in motion, but now wasn't the time to let Kelli in on the surprise. The time would come soon enough. Like her adversary the Devil, Stuart was setting the trap to *devour* Kelli.

It was 10:30 by the time they stepped outside of the warmth of the restaurant and into the chilled winds. Even in the wintertime, tourists could still be seen walking up and down Beach Boulevard.

"Thanks for listening," Kelli said as they reached the door of her car.

"No thanks necessary," Stuart told her. "Are you okay now?" he asked. "If you're not ready to go home yet, we can take a walk. I don't want you to feel as though I'm rushing you if you need more time," he said.

"No," Kelli assured him. "I need to get on home. I'm sure if Jhordan isn't there already, he'll be home shortly."

Stuart held the car door open for her and Kelli got inside. Her lack of sleep over the past few nights was catching up with her. She felt tired, and even though she knew it was a possibility that Jhordan wouldn't get home until long after midnight, she was ready to end her night with Stuart and get home. Between her talk with her father and the prayer that they prayed in the Upper Room, she felt increasingly uncomfortable in the lawyer's presence, though he gave her no valid reason to.

"Call me if you need me," he said as he continued to stand beside her car. "I'll check on you next week," he said, then closed the door beside her.

Stuart watched silently as Kelli's car pulled from the parking lot and onto Beach Boulevard. A smile crossed his face as she drove out of sight. *Just one more week,* he thought to himself. *Just one more week.*

12

PROMISES
BEYOND JORDAN

They'd arrived at church at separate times and in separate vehicles. This time it wasn't because of Jhordan's work schedule, but because he'd overslept, and Kelli hadn't bothered to wake him as he slept on the couch in the living room. Instead, she'd dressed herself and walked right past him on her way out the front door to attend Sunday morning services.

The woman who had been occupying the seat on the end of the pew next to Kelli graciously gave it up when she saw Jhordan walk in the church while the choir sang. When the song ended and they were all seated, Jazmin waved enthusiastically at her father. Jhordan returned her smile and winked at her, but he also noted Kelli's demeanor. He knew that she was very aware that he was sitting next to her, but she didn't acknowledge his arrival.

Last night he beat her home, and her absence took him by surprise. Where was she, and why wasn't she at home? he'd planned to ask, but he'd already fallen asleep before she arrived. When he finally woke up this morning, he was at first unsure that she'd come home at all until he walked into their bedroom and saw the covers pulled back and the gown she'd worn thrown over the bedpost. It was probably a good thing that he'd been asleep when she'd arrived. How could he have asked her of her whereabouts when he was seldom at home?

Dressed in a hot-pink dress that made his heart skip a beat, Kelli was a lovely sight, as always. Her hair was pinned up in the back, and a portion of her silky locks were set free in the front so that they fell to a straight bang alongside her face, partially covering her left cheek.

Jhordan struggled to focus as Pastor Berry finally stood at the podium and opened his Bible. He directed them to a Scripture, and Jhordan turned to it as instructed, but his mind was preoccupied by a burst of mingled emotions.

From his side vision, he followed the trail that led from the three-inch heels of her black pumps all the way up to the point where her knees crossed each other and became a stand on which to balance her Bible. He could see the softness of her freshly shaved legs through the sheer stockings that enveloped them.

Jhordan watched as Kelli fumbled with the wedding set that he'd placed on her finger just over ten months ago—twisting it in one direction and then the other, like a nervous child. At one point, she slipped it from her finger, and he felt a strong pounding in his chest. For a moment, it seemed as though she was going to hand it to him. Instead, she replaced it and continued rotating it as she followed along with the Scripture references.

Kelli was a woman who was very conscious of her appearance. Everything about her was so feminine and so delicate. Jhordan loved that. He looked at her hands and found himself longing to touch them. Visions of her snatching her hands away because of his lack of affection and attention over the past weeks—months even—kept his hands glued beneath his Bible.

The "turn to your neighbor" commands had begun long ago. Kelli never looked in his direction. Jazmin became her constant connection to relay all of the given messages to. Being that he was sitting at the edge of the pew, Jhordan had no one else to look to, so he stared straight into the pages of the Book in front of him and said nothing.

A half hour after beginning his sermon, Pastor Berry was finished, and Jhordan had hardly heard a word that he'd said. For a brief moment as he saw Kelli looking ahead at the pastor in the pulpit, Jhordan wondered if she was wishing that she'd married the man who had briefly been her high school sweetheart. Their breakup wasn't a bitter one. Winston Berry had been a senior and Kelli a sophomore. They'd been dating less than a year when he went away for college. The distance between them physically eventually built an emotional gap as well, and they'd amicably decided to part ways. Jhordan hated thinking that wishful thinking was playing a part in her look of fixation.

After all the other church business was taken care of and the benediction given, the congregation began dispersing. Kelli purposely turned her back to him as she gathered her belongings. The hot-pink outfit looked even better from the rear.

"You were asleep when Ms. Kelli left," Jazmin announced as she climbed into his arms for a big bear hug.

"I know," he said. "Daddy was kind of tired."

"That's what Ms. Kelli said," she told him while sliding from his grasp and onto the floor. "Can I go play with the twins?" she turned to Kelli and asked.

"Sure, baby," Kelli said. "I'll be over in a minute."

"Are you angry at me?" Jhordan asked Kelli softly after she'd gathered all of her things.

She didn't immediately answer him, but he saw a look in her eyes that spoke volumes. It didn't exactly come across as anger, but more like a mixture of hurt, confusion, and regret. She had reason to feel all three, but it was the third one that hit him the hardest.

"No," she finally spoke. "I'm not angry at you."

Even in her despondent state, she was beautiful. Jhordan could see his own reflection in her brown eyes. His heart raced, and his fingertips tingled. He wanted to pull her so closely to him that he'd be able to feel her body inside of his. He wanted to kiss her so deeply that he'd be able to taste the peppermint that he knew she'd eaten before entering the church doors.

She had no idea the effect she had on him. He wanted to say and do so many things, but instead he took a step backward and handed her the purse that had fallen from her shoulder during their lengthy eye lock. He had to get himself together. He couldn't leave and go home to her feeling this defenseless and vulnerable.

"Uh," Jhordan stammered, "why don't you and Jazmin go to your mom's for dinner?" he said. "I have some things to take care of."

"Some *things?*" she asked.

"Yeah." Jhordan nodded.

"Fine," Kelli said casually as she edged past him. "Tell her I said hello."

Momentarily, Jhordan froze at his wife's words. Too stunned to speak, he watched in silence while she worked her way through the crowd until she disappeared from his view.

"Oh, no," he whispered as he sank back onto the seat.

The minutes ticked away on the clock. The church sanctuary generally emptied rather quickly following services so the cleaning crew could do their job before locking the doors. The sound of a vacuum cleaner signaled that the tidying had already begun. Jhordan was unfazed. He stared at the blue carpeted floors beneath his feet, replaying Kelli's words over and over again in his head.

"Jhordan?"

He heard his name called, but Jhordan didn't look up from his gaze.

"Jhordan," Pastor Berry called again. "Are you okay?"

"I'm fine." His response was little more than a whisper.

Pastor Berry unapologetically wedged his bulky frame into the limited space between Jhordan and the armrest that marked the end of the pew—forcing Jhordan to move over to give him room. Taking off the tie that he'd worn during the service and placing it on his lap, Pastor Berry turned to face him.

"Jhordan," he began, "I can't help you if you won't let me."

"I don't need your help." His quivering voice lacked the tone of certainty that it carried when he'd spoken the same words to Dr. Ellis just weeks earlier.

"You'll notice that I didn't *ask* you whether or not you needed my help," the pastor came back in an almost fatherly manner. "Now, let's start over," he said. "Are you okay?"

Jhordan finally looked up and momentarily allowed his eyes to meet those of the man he'd never before spoken to in a private setting. His distrust chilled him, and reservation took over. Swallowing, he looked away and clinched his jaws as though forcing himself not to talk.

"Okay then," Pastor Berry said as he removed his shoes and stretched his legs out in front of him. "I'm a patient man, and I ain't in no hurry. What about you?"

"I have to go," Jhordan said as he stood and began walking away.

"Last winter, I married the two of you," he said, stopping him in his tracks. "Another winter hasn't even ended yet, but something has happened to turn your marriage as cold as ice. Why don't we start right there?" he said with an invitational pat to the cushion beside him.

Jhordan's legs seemed to have taken on a will of their own. His mind was directing them to make a beeline to the door, but instead, they led him back to the seat that he'd just left moments earlier. The two of them sat for several minutes without talking.

"Edward," Pastor Berry called to the man who was still cleaning the church. "Just leave all that stuff right there—furniture spray, rags, and all. I'll make sure it gets finished before next Sunday. You just go on home. Thank you."

The custodian left and was replaced by a strange silence that blanketed the room. True to his word, the pastor sat patiently and gave no indication that he was pressed with any other issues.

Jhordan sat confused as to how to handle the uncomfortable situation he was in. The only reason he'd allowed Winston Berry to preside over their marriage ceremony was because her family insisted. He'd thought it was awkward, but Kelli and the minister's courtship, according to them, had been long forgotten, and they now only had a pastor/member relationship. The fact that Pastor Berry had a wife of his own helped, but besides that,

Jhordan had developed an unexplainable confidence in the preacher upon his first visit to the church, long before he had become aware of Winston's past involvement with Kelli. Since that time, Pastor Berry had given him no reason to distrust.

"Maybe I can help get the ball rolling," the preacher said. "This has something to do with Kelli, and it's something that you don't wish to discuss with me because I have a history with her. How am I doing so far?"

Jhordan continued his downward stare.

"You don't think I can be impartial?" Pastor Berry asked.

Only a year or two separated their ages. That was another excuse that Jhordan used for choosing to confide in Dr. Ellis. His father had always taught him that wisdom came with age, and if that was the case, Winston knew little more about how to handle his situation than he did. Yet, today, for the first time, Jhordan felt a desire to open up to the man and take his chances. Nothing else had seemed to work, and with Kelli thinking he was seeing another woman, it was a certainty that she was on her way out of his life. At this point, Jhordan felt he had nothing to lose.

Jhordan finally spoke after the passing of several more minutes. "She thinks I'm having an affair."

"Are you?"

"Of course not," Jhordan said through a pronounced grimace.

"Why does she think you're having an affair?"

"I don't know."

"Have you given her any reason to *believe* that you might be having an affair?"

"No," Jhordan said. "I mean, I haven't been around

much," he admitted, "but that's no reason to think I'm being unfaithful."

"Really?" Pastor Berry asked. "Where've you been?"

"Here and there," he said with a childlike shrug.

"That's two real good reasons to believe you're having an affair, Jhordan. You been *here* and you been *there*, but you haven't been at home. Come on, Jhordan—talk to me, brotha to brotha. Whatever you say stays right here," he promised. "I've known Kelli for a lot of years, and you know that. She *can't* be driving you away, can she?"

"Yes, she is," he said.

"How?" Pastor Berry said. "She was so happy to be marrying you. She was in tears when she showed me her engagement ring the day after you proposed. She had so much love for you. Has all of that changed already?"

"No." Jhordan sighed in frustration. "Nobody understands me," he said. "It's meaningless to talk about this—especially to a man who's always had a good marriage."

"Is that right?" Pastor Berry sat up straight. "Let me tell you something 'bout this man that maybe you don't know," he said as he pointed at himself. "All you see is what you see when I'm standing in that pulpit on Sundays, but I've been through a lot in my years.

"I know you went through a divorce. I may not know the reasons, but the reasons don't even matter as far as I'm concerned. No, I've never been through a divorce, but I watched my mother go through one that caused her about as much pain as the marriage did. My father was bigger than I am. My mom is less than five feet tall. The man she loved put her in the hospital on a number of occasions. He not only abused her, but I still have scars to show what he did to me."

Winston pointed at an area near his left ear where stitches once were. Jhordan never would have imagined that the man who preached God's Word every Sunday morning had once been the abused son of a battered mother. His revelation got Jhordan's full attention.

"Winston Berry Sr. was a crooked, domineering lowlife that my mom was naïve enough to marry when my grandmama clearly warned her of what would happen if she did," he continued. "He beat his family with the same hands that, as a police officer, he used to arrest other men who beat their wives and children. The love he should have been giving to my mama, he gave to my aunt instead.

"Due to enduring constant beatings, my mother lost her ability to have children, but I ended up with a cousin who was also my stepsister. I know about hurt and pain, Jhordan. I know about loving somebody and wanting them to love you back, but getting nothing in return but constant hurt. Don't tell me what I won't understand. You might be surprised."

"I'm sorry," Jhordan said, overwhelmed by what he'd just heard.

"And you know what else I understand," he added. "I understand that even when you move on or grow up, the hurt is still there. But you know what? You got to move on or else the hurt will keep you in captivity your whole life. I had to learn that for myself."

"Kelli never told me about that," Jhordan said. "I had no idea."

"She couldn't tell you what she didn't know," Pastor Berry said. "You're the first person in this church that I've ever disclosed that information to. Now, let me be the first person you trust with *your* story."

He still cringed at the idea, but slowly and cautiously,

Jhordan opened up and uncovered the details that had followed him from childhood to manhood. He'd never shared with anyone the whole story, and he'd never expected Pastor Berry to be the first to hear it all. The more he talked, the more he wanted to talk. Just telling the preacher and watching him as he listened without interruption and without judgment made his heart feel lighter than it had in years. By the time he finished, Jhordan was near tears but managed to withhold them successfully.

"Is it worth losing everything, Jhordan?" Pastor Berry asked after he'd ended in silence. "God gave you another chance at the family that you thought you once had. Are you going to allow fear to control you to the point of making you lose it all?"

"I can't go through that again," Jhordan said while shaking his head. "I cried so many nights after my separation and ultimate divorce from Sadonia that I could build a river of nothing but my tears," Jhordan said. "I can't do it again."

"Jhordan, God has so much for you, but it's on hold because you're standing in your own way," Pastor Berry said. "You're hanging on to every hurt, disappointment, and fear you've ever encountered.

"There is a river in the Bible that shares your name, called Jordan River," he said. "In Deuteronomy, Moses prayed and asked God to let him go over and see the good land that was *beyond* Jordan. Don't you see? Moses knew that God had promises beyond Jordan, and you have to know that He has promises beyond *Jhordan*," he said, pointing in Jhordan's direction as he ministered to him.

"You've got your own river that was built with your tears, and instead of crossing it, you're standing in the middle of it—nursing it and refusing to let God's sunshine dry it up. It ain't nothing but a river, but you're making it an ocean, and the shorelines are getting farther and farther away. You have to stop dwelling on Jhordan and his hurts, his failures and letdowns. Yes, you've experienced a lot of horrible things in your life—unimaginable hurts, even. But it's not about Jhordan, and it's not about the river of tears that you've shed.

"By your actions you're telling God that you'd rather be alone than to share your life with a woman who truly loves you. You're telling Him that you'd rather be alone than with a woman you love so much that just the thought of sharing an intimate moment with her makes you perspire. You're telling Him that you don't care how much your daughter loves the mother He's given her; you'd rather her feel the pain of being motherless like you did as a child.

"Well, it's time for you to get beyond Jhordan," he said. "You need to go to your wife and tell her *everything*. It's the only way that your actions since marrying her can be explained. God is a loving, kind, and patient God, Jhordan, but He's not going to continue to make Kelli suffer because of your stubbornness and disobedience. She's His child too."

Jhordan sat silently and returned his gaze to the carpet under his feet. Winston was right. His words had been nothing new. It was the same thing that Dr. Ellis and Jeanette had already told him, but Pastor Berry's words combined with his experience had opened Jhordan's eyes in a way that theirs hadn't.

"Let's pray a short prayer together," the minister said as he covered Jhordan's hand with his. "Then we can sit here and talk some more for as long as you want. We can pray some more too. I told you before—I'm in no hurry. When you leave me, I want you to go straight home and start working on salvaging your relationship with your wife."

Kelli lay awake in her bed and looked at the clock on her nightstand. It was nearing midnight. The talk between Jhordan and Pastor Berry that began at 3:30 in the afternoon had gone late into the night hours. The pastor had called less than half an hour ago to let her know that Jhordan had been in a lengthy meeting with him that included dinner and was just heading home.

She wanted to know details, but the pastor didn't give her the opportunity to ask about them. Hearing the front door open and shut, she closed her eyes and pretended to be asleep. She heard the keys drop into the ceramic bowl that sat on the table in the living room.

Thinking that he'd do as usual and make his bed there on the sofa, Kelli was caught unprepared at the sound of the bedroom door opening. Keeping her eyes shut, she held her breath as she felt Jhordan standing over her body. She heard him walk to the opposite side of the bed and slowly remove his shoes. He was still fully dressed when she felt him slide next to her under the covers.

Carefully, so as not to wake her, he slipped one arm around her and came to a rest with his lips next to her ear. The feel of his warm breath against the side of her face sent chills racing through her body.

"I'm sorry, sweetheart," he whispered. "I'm so sorry."

13

A LOVE
SO STRONG

Good morning, Kelli. You could answer your cell
phone *sometimes*," Sasha said as she walked into
the bookstore carrying a box so big she could barely see
over it.

"What's all of that?" Kelli snapped from the daze
she'd been in and rushed to clear a spot on the counter for
the unexpected, oversized delivery.

"It's all those teddy bears we ordered last month.
Somehow the warehouse shipped them to my home ad-
dress instead of here to the store. I need to make some
phone calls today for all those customers who ordered
them and have been waiting. But you'd know that if you
listened to your cell messages once in a while."

"Sorry," Kelli apologized. "I've been so busy and preoccupied with other stuff. I think my cell phone is in my
briefcase, which has been in the trunk of my car all weekend."

"Preoccupied with what other stuff? Is this still about Jhordan? What did that fool attorney tell you this time?"

"This has nothing to do with Stuart," Kelli told her. "I don't need him to tell me that something is wrong. I'm smart enough to figure that one out on my own."

"What's going on now?" Sasha took a quick look around to be sure early shoppers hadn't come in. "You guys still aren't having sex?"

"It's not just about that, Sasha." Kelli carefully cut open the sealed box as she spoke. "I've gotten used to being the celibate wife."

"It hasn't been *that* long, Kelli."

"It's been a month, Sasha," she said. "That's far too long. But I'm not worried about that anymore," Kelli lied, "really I'm not. I don't even want Jhordan putting his hands on me anymore."

"What?" Sasha's eyes stretched to capacity at her friend's words. "You're just saying that now because of what's going on between you and him."

"Well, let's just say that I can't imagine having a desire for him again, Sasha."

"I understand that you're running out of patience with his behavior, but even with that, I can't understand why you wouldn't want—"

"He's having an affair, Sasha!"

A thick hush overshadowed the room. Saying those words to Sasha ignited Kelli's emotions, and tears flowed from her eyes like a broken dam. Kelli hated the fact that she even cared one way or another. She'd always said that the quickest way to get her to fall out of love was to find out that the one she loved was being unfaithful. Now, although she wanted to be able to be immediately detached, she found herself eating her own words.

"Do you know for sure?" Sasha whispered with a touch to her friend's hand. "Did you find proof that he was seeing someone else?"

"Yes." Kelli's tears seemed to choke her as she spoke. "I mean, I don't have proof," she said, "but I do know for sure."

"How?"

If history was any indication, shoppers would be arriving shortly; but Sasha needed to hear the whole story. As much as she knew that Kelli wouldn't fabricate a story concerning her husband, she couldn't help but believe that somehow her friend was mistaken. Jhordan wouldn't . . . *couldn't* be the man Kelli was beginning to think he was.

"What other answer is there for his absenteeism?" Kelli asked. She wiped more tears as she continued talking. "I barely saw him all weekend, and I'm tired of making excuses for him to Jazmin."

"Is that it?" Sasha said. "That's been going on for a while, Kelli. What's happened that's any different from the previous weeks and months? Why are you so sure now that his behavior is linked to an affair?"

"Because last night I think he confessed the whole thing to Winston. I know he had a long meeting with him, and I think that's what it was about. I'm almost sure of it, Sasha. I knew that Winston wouldn't tell me about it because of confidentiality. He wasn't going to break Jhordan's confidence, and by the time he made it home, I just pretended to be asleep."

"Why?"

"Because I knew he'd been talking to our pastor, and I wasn't prepared for him to walk in the house and come clean with me about the whole situation. I know both the personal and ministerial sides to Pastor Berry. Either side would have told Jhordan that honesty was the only way to handle this mess. I just didn't want to hear it, Sasha," Kelli explained. "I didn't want to hear him say the words."

"So, what happened?"

"He got in bed with me, and he kept whispering to me how sorry he was."

"Sorry for what?"

"The affair, Sasha."

"Did you at least ask him about it this morning?"

"Yeah, right," Kelli said with a mocking laugh. "Jhordan wasn't even home when I got up. He'd already left the house—probably to meet *her*. He said he was sorry. He didn't say he wasn't going to see her anymore."

"How do you know?" Sasha insisted. "Maybe he was sorry for something totally different."

"Like what?" Kelli said.

"I don't know, but you can't just go straight for thinking the worst thing imaginable. Have some faith in him, Kelli."

"You think I *want* to be right about this?" New tears slowly found their way down her already moist cheeks. "Do you know how much I love that man, Sasha? Do you know how hard this is for me? I'm a newlywed. I married a man, and then I wasn't enough to keep him satisfied. Do you know how that makes me—"

Kelli's sentence was cut short. Both women turned as they realized they were no longer alone. Sasha's face reddened with embarrassment, and Kelli tried unsuccessfully to wipe away the tears that continued flowing even after she stopped speaking.

"Greetings." No smile accompanied the solemn salutation that Jhordan extended to the unprepared women.

"Hey, Jhordan," Sasha mumbled with a forced brief smile.

"Can you do this alone for a while?" Jhordan asked her. "I need to take Kelli away. Please," he added after noting Sasha's guarded hesitation.

"Sure," she finally said with a shrug. "Take all the time you need."

Slowly responding to her husband's hand motions, Kelli silently rounded the corner and glanced over her shoulder at her best friend before following Jhordan out the door and into the parking lot. She hugged her jacket close and swallowed back what felt like a waterfall of tears that begged to be released as she climbed into his truck.

"Just where are you taking me?"

"Please just give me a chance," Jhordan pleaded.

"Jhordan, that's the problem. I've given you so much, and you haven't reciprocated."

Kelli's mind raced as she stared out the window at nothing in particular. Even as they pulled into the driveway of her parents' home, the scenery looked unfamiliar in her clouded vision. As Jhordan shut off the engine of the truck and got out, she continued to sit in a daze of heartbreak and confusion.

"Come," he said softly after opening the door for her and extending a hand to help her step from her seat.

"What in the world are we doing here?"

Wesley looked from one dreary face to the other when he answered Jhordan's knock. After acknowledging his son-in-law, he stepped aside to allow them into the living room. Kelli's tears pressed harder when she felt her father's comforting arms around her. She felt safe and protected for a moment, but it disappeared as soon as he released her.

Still standing near the doorway, she noticed that all of her immediate family had been summoned to watch the falling of the ax. Tony and Cheryl each cradled a sleeping twin in their arms as they sat on the loveseat. Her mother sat on the arm of Wesley's favorite recliner and sipped hot coffee from a ceramic mug. Someone had even picked Jazmin up from school.

Sitting alone on the couch, the girl offered a smile but looked on with concerned eyes as her stepmother sank onto the cushions beside her. Kelli's legs felt weak and unable to uphold the weight of her body any longer. She watched as Jhordan slowly removed the leather bomber jacket that she'd bought for him during their courtship, revealing a long-sleeved sweater that showed the incredible build that lately she'd only been able to admire from a distance.

Lord, have mercy! For a moment, a different sensation took a front seat inside of Kelli, but the reality of it all quickly set back in when Jhordan sat beside her and stared at his clasped hands. For what felt like hours, no one spoke. Kelli looked at no one's face. Instead, she stared at the beautifully decorated gifts that lay beneath her parents' tree that would be opened in just two days.

A part of her wanted to throw her body at Jhordan's feet and beg him not to confess. Kelli tried to put forth a brave front for herself and her family, but inside she was dying while attempting to prepare herself for Jhordan's confession to her and her family about the other woman in his life, this woman whom he'd been spending his nights with while she slept alone.

The extended silence in the room was too much for Kelli. The waiting was more tormenting than the end result would be. With trembling hands and another batch of tears, she removed the wedding set he'd put on her finger and placed it on the table in front of him. Rising from her seat, she spoke in a shaky voice.

"You don't have to say anything. I'll save you the trouble." Her intent to run into her parents' bedroom and lock herself inside was hampered by the strong hand that solidly grabbed her arm.

"Kelli," Jhordan said in an almost frantic whisper. "No, baby. Please don't walk out. Let's talk about this."

"About what, Jhordan?" she said through heavy sobs. Wesley stopped Mary as she prepared to rush to her daughter's side.

"Kelli, hear the boy out," her father called to her.

"I trusted you!" Kelli yelled—disregarding her father's instructions. "You told me you loved me. How could you do this to me? You let me fall in love with you and Jazmin, and now you want to take it all away," she continued, ignoring Jhordan's attempts to quiet her.

"Well, I give up. I've tried to be a good wife and a good mother. I've prayed and I've cried. I've asked God why, and He hasn't answered me. I can't handle this anymore, Jhordan! I know what you're here to say. I'm just saying it first. I guess I should have taken the cue when you said I could leave a month ago. I guess I'm a little slow at getting it, but I get it now. You don't have to leave," she sobbed. "I will."

"Ms. Kelli, please don't leave," Jazmin begged tearfully as she grabbed Kelli around her waist. "Please don't leave, Mommy. Please don't leave!"

Mommy. The word tapped into the reserves of Kelli's soul.

"How could you *do* this to us?" she said with a punch to Jhordan's chest that she was sure was more painful to her hand than it was to him.

"Sweetheart—" he interrupted attempting to stop her again.

"How could you marry me if I didn't mean any more

to you than this? I *waited* for you, Jhordan," she said. "I gave myself to you, and you turned it into a joke! You could have spit in my face in a crowded restaurant, and I wouldn't be any more humiliated than I am right now."

"Sweetheart." Jhordan finally silenced her by placing three fingers on her lips. "Shhh," he added when she made an attempt to speak again.

Kelli saw sadness—maybe even fear—in his dark eyes. He let out a heavy sigh as though overwhelmed by her speech before slipping his hand from her lips and gently pulling her back into a seated position.

"Come over here with Grandmama, sugar," Mary instructed Jazmin, who seemed traumatized by the events of the recent minutes. Kelli watched while her mother hugged Jazmin close. She'd never heard her refer to herself as Jazmin's grandmother before.

"I am so, so sorry," Jhordan said as he shook his head slowly. "Until yesterday, I was unaware that you thought there was another woman in my life. When you said what you said to me at church, I couldn't believe my ears. And to hear you now . . ." he continued. "I'm sorry I put you through this. There is no other woman, baby."

"Jhordan, don't lie to me," Kelli started in a tone of disbelief.

"Please," Jhordan implored, "let me speak."

He looked at the concerned faces of all of his in-laws who sat around them before returning his attention to Kelli. He'd already spent the early hours of the morning convincing them that he was faithful to his marriage despite Kelli's legitimate concerns. Still, there was so much more to tell.

"There is no other woman in my life, sweetheart," he reiterated. "I lived that, remember? I know the pain of loving someone and having them turn out to be a deceptive liar. I would *never* impose that kind of hurt on another. I couldn't do it to my worst enemy, let alone you."

Kelli sat silently and searched her husband's face for any signs of dishonesty. "If you're not having an affair, Jhordan, how do you explain your actions? You won't touch me, you won't sleep in the same bed with me, and you're never at home. The last time we were getting ready to—" she started.

"I know," Jhordan stopped her. "I never should have walked out on you like that. I didn't know what else to do. I'm sorry."

"I don't want you to tell me you're sorry, Jhordan. What I want—what I *need*—is an explanation. Tell me why you don't want to be with me. Tell me what's been going on with you."

"Sweetheart, those nights I was away, I was either in private counseling sessions with Dr. Ellis at Mount Nebo or just sitting in some vacant lot in my truck like a homeless fool. Believe me when I tell you that I so want to be with you."

His words sounded sweet, but they only heightened Kelli's confusion. "Then I don't understand."

"Give me five minutes, and I'll tell you everything," Jhordan promised. "This isn't easy for me to talk about, but I need to tell all of you. I should have told *you*"—he looked at Kelli—"a long time ago, and for not doing so, I apologize. I know that doesn't take away the misery I've caused, but it's all I can offer right now."

His requested five minutes stretched into nearly half an hour as Jhordan painfully told Kelli and her family the full story of his life. Everybody knew that he'd witnessed his mother's suicide, but nobody knew of the moments before the horrible shooting when she had told him that he was the reason she was doing it. He had later found that the depression his mother had suffered with for years had started after his birth; that hadn't made the blow any softer. Because she had never sought medication for it, her illness had never gotten better. Though he had been told over and over again that he wasn't at fault, the combination of the timing of her condition and her words had left a guilt he could never fully shake.

Jhordan had never told anyone how he'd felt as though he was the reason for his mother's instability. He'd never told anyone how, for years, he had hated his mother for declaring her love for him just before pulling the trigger.

As painful as it was for him to tell the complete tragic story of his mother, it was the fresher wounds of the unedited version of his failed marriage to Sadonia that caused a slow trickle of tears to escape from the corners of his eyes.

There was so much more to the saga than anyone had ever been made aware of. Sadonia's affair had been brought to light when the second child she'd given birth to was stricken with a rare heart disease. Jazmin had been only eleven months old at the time. Kelli gasped at his revelation. It was the first she'd heard about a son.

"He was beautiful." Jhordan smiled slightly as he reminisced. "He looked just like his mother." Despite all of the medical attempts, Jhoshua, as Jhordan had named him, died when he was only five months old.

In the process of running tests during the frantic attempts to save the infant's life, the doctors had drawn blood from both Sadonia and Jhordan. The result of those blood tests started unraveling the facts that would shatter Jhordan's world. With little remorse and what seemed to be a relief that she no longer had to hide her transgressions, Sadonia had admitted her secret life with the childhood sweetheart whom she'd never really stopped loving.

Jhordan had loved her and said he'd forgive her if she'd just put an end to the affair and go through counseling with him at the church they attended. She had responded by aggressively twisting the knife she'd already jabbed into his back. Telling Jhordan that her lover was also Jazmin's father and that she wanted a divorce so that she could make them a real family had been more than Jhordan could take.

For weeks during the divorce proceedings, he had wallowed in self-pity—even contemplated suicide—not knowing how to handle the deadly mixture of anger, hatred, and heartbreak. As in the case with his mother, the last thing Sadonia had said to him as she packed her things and moved herself and Jazmin into a condominium that she'd share with him was "You're the reason I'm doing this."

She'd told Jhordan that if he had just gone to college as she'd been trying to get him to do and gotten a job paying more money so that they could live in the more expensive neighborhoods of New York, she would have never allowed Peter back into her life. Still declaring her love for him, she had walked out of their home and out of his life—taking the child he loved with her.

A few months later, after finding out that Jazmin was in fact Jhordan's biological child, Peter had insisted that she relinquish her parental rights. Not wanting the responsibility of raising another man's child, he'd issued the staunch ultimatum. Losing the three-and-a-half-carat diamond on her finger and the rights to unlimited shopping at all of her favorite stores had been too big of a sacrifice. Instead, Sadonia had handed the child to Jhordan to rear alone.

"She saved my life," Jhordan whispered with a loving look toward his daughter. "Jazmin saved my life. I had prayed so hard for a reason to live, and God gave me my baby back."

Kelli had had no idea the magnitude of suffering her husband had endured at the hands of the women he loved and trusted the most. She had never been told about the dead baby he had thought was his or the enormity of Sadonia's callousness toward him. No wonder he wanted nothing to do with her. The fact that he allowed Jazmin to remain a part of her birth mother's life gave Kelli a new respect for the spiritual strength he possessed. He put Jazmin's total well-being before his own issues with her mother.

"Every woman I've ever given my heart to has crushed it, Kelli." Jhordan turned his total attention to his wife. "My mother killed herself the week of Christmas. Sadonia walked out two days before Christmas. The closer it got to Christmas, the more insecure I felt in our relationship.

"I promised to never fully give my heart to another woman. That's why I haven't been around. I didn't mean to hurt you, Kelli," he said. "I was just trying to protect myself."

"Do you love me?" Kelli asked. She needed to hear him speak the words.

"I'm—" Jhordan's lips trembled, and his voice was barely above a whisper as he spoke the words he'd never admitted. "I'm scared."

"Jhordan—" Kelli started.

"I have a love so strong for you that I have to run from you in order to have a fighting chance at guarding my heart from what feels like the inevitable," Jhordan answered. "I can't lie to you, sweetheart. That scares me to death."

Kelli stood and pulled him close—burying her face in his chest and holding him in a long embrace. It had been a long time since she'd felt his body so closely meshed to hers. She could live with his fears and insecurities. Jhordan's declared love for her was all she needed to hear.

14

ALL CRACKED UP

The door to the corner office slammed shut, and Maya and Stephanie looked across the room at each other. The two gossiping secretaries who ran the front office of McMillian At Law shook their heads as they peered in the direction of Stuart's closed door.

Though more than twenty years separated the two administrative assistants, they got along well—both sharing a gift for gab and a love for drama. Fifty-two-year-old Stephanie peered over her reading glasses from the boxes where she was packing away the holiday decorations.

"Wonder what's with him?" she asked. "He been acting like that for four or five days now."

"I don't know," Maya said with a rolling of her neck, "but he *needs* to go back to Atlanta with all them other bourgeois Negroes that's trying to be something they ain't. He gettin' on my last nerve, and he 'bout to get cussed out. How 'bout he didn't even give us a Christmas bonus like the other partners did?" Maya pointed out. "And he got the nerve to talk to me like I'm his *personal* secretary."

"What did he just say to you?" Stephanie pried for more.

"He asked if he'd gotten any phone calls," Maya said. "I gave him his messages, and he looked through them and got irritated. Apparently, he didn't get the call he was looking for. Probably some airhead he been messing with done dropped him."

"Good," Stephanie said unsympathetically. "He come here from Atlanta and probably thought all the girls here would be knocking his door down. Ain't nobody stud'in' him."

"What it *is*, see," Maya explained as they drew in close together and continued speaking with lowered voices, "is that girl who was calling here almost every day for him done stopped calling. They must have had a fight or something, 'cause she ain't called none this week, I know. She had stopped calling *before* Christmas, and she ain't called since we opened back up."

"What y'all call that?" Stephanie asked with a laugh. "Is that what they mean when they say the playa done been played?"

"His phone line just lit up," Maya pointed out as the two of them gathered at her desk and watched the glow of the button as though an egg were about to hatch. "I bet you he's calling her again."

"I'd trade my paycheck to be a fly on his wall right now," Stephanie said. "I wonder who she is and what he's saying."

"Whatever it is," Maya said, "I guarantee you, he's lying."

Behind the closed door, Stuart tightened his jaws and

clinched his fist as he once again listened to the voice mail message on Kelli's cellular telephone.

"Kelli, this is Stuart," he said, trying to suppress the anger that was brewing inside of him. "I haven't heard from you in a few days, and this is the fourth time that I'm leaving you a message. I have a gift for you. Give me a call today at the office or on my cell. Bye."

Releasing a lung full of air, he stopped the force of his arm just before what would have been a slamming down of the telephone. Two and a half weeks ago, he'd put in for next week to be his vacation. The white sands and warm breezes of Daytona Beach awaited. He'd made sure that his time-share suite that overlooked the waters was secured just for the occasion.

He'd taken it slow—played his cards just right—lined all his ducks in a careful row. Everything was going according to plan, and now . . . something had gone wrong. In each of their private meetings, Stuart had been careful not to overplay his hand. He had never said an outright negative word about Jhordan or pointed accusing fingers at him for his open avoidance of Kelli. He'd wanted to—but he never had.

As the strain had grown greater between the man he'd never met but hated and the woman he desired, Stuart never crossed the line. He gained Kelli's trust, allowed her to cry in his arms, offered friendly advice, and sat up late at night and talked to her by telephone when her husband had once again abandoned the home without a valid reason.

"Is this the thanks I get?" Stuart whispered harshly as he stared at the telephone he'd just put down.

He wished he knew what was going on. Today was the day he'd marked on his calendar as the perfect day to convince Kelli to take a trip with him. The holiday was over; most likely, she'd gotten no gift from her two-timing husband, and she'd need him now more than ever. The diamond necklace he had bought for her sat in a gift box on his desk.

Stuart had planned to tell her that a trip would be a great way to clear her head and get away from the pressures of her troubled marriage. In her state of mind, he knew that he could persuade her to go along with him. He'd already succeeded in making her comfortable and letting down her guard. The hard part was behind him.

Once in Daytona Beach, he'd become everything that Jhordan wasn't. Neither hell nor high water would divert his attention away from her. He'd give her all the adoration that she'd been starving for over the months. Kelli's beautiful body had barely been touched since marrying Jhordan Adams. Stuart had plans to rectify that as well. Even good little "church girls" needed love and affection. He could take her mind away from principles and convictions. Those things that she viewed as wrong he'd make *feel* so right that she'd give in to new passions that he'd awaken in her. The airline tickets that were to take them to a land of ecstasy lay in plain view in an envelope in his inbox.

Pounding a clinched fist on his desk and simultaneously uttering an angry oath, Stuart stood from his chair and shoved his hands in his pants pockets while staring out of his office window. He'd planned everything too perfectly to give up now. He had to find out why his calls had gone unanswered.

Sasha watched her friend hang up the phone and noted the soft curl of her lips. She couldn't help but enjoy the moment, remembering days when Kelli's smiles were either forced or phony.

"That is Jhordan's third time today calling you, and it's only noon."

"He was supposed to get off at three today," Kelli said. "He just called and said that they've asked him to work a double shift. That means he won't get off 'til eleven. I would be disappointed, but that actually works in my favor today since I have some running around to do after work."

"So, do you feel like a newlywed again?"

Kelli's grin broadened as she nodded her head. Due to natural circumstances out of her control, this month's timing of Jhordan's confession had not allowed them the opportunity to enjoy each other's company in the most intimate way. However, today was a new day, and plans were already in motion to make tonight as memorable as possible.

Kelli felt an excitement inside of her that she'd not experienced in months. Just in time for their first Christmas together, she and Jhordan had found new reasons to celebrate. For the past few nights, regardless of their limitations, Kelli had enjoyed the warmth of her husband's body beside hers. She'd taken pleasure in going to sleep and waking up in his arms.

Tonight, with no drawn boundaries, she'd made plans for a special evening. Since it was the end of the week and school was out until after the New Year, Wesley and Mary had agreed to allow Jazmin to spend the night at their home. Although Friday was their busiest day for business, and last-minute shoppers sometimes forced them to stay open late, Kelli had no intentions of being at the bookstore a minute past 6:00 p.m.

From her own store's stock, she'd already bagged several vanilla-scented candles and a popular milk-based bubble bath that was legendary for leaving the skin soft and smooth to the touch. With one stop to make on the way home, she should be able to walk through her front door by 7:00 p.m. at the latest, And with Jhordan working the late shift, she'd have plenty of time to get everything ready for his arrival.

"I guess Attorney McMillian wasn't too pleased to hear that you and Jhordan had made up," Sasha said, marring the adoring picture that had formed in Kelli's head.

"I haven't talked to Stuart," Kelli said. "Not in the past week I just kind of decided to cut him off cold turkey. He was a good listener, but Daddy got bad vibes without even meeting him."

"*Daddy* got bad vibes?" Sasha planted both her hands on her wide hips and faced Kelli. "I'm the one who told you he was bad news from the very beginning," she said. "How come you didn't cut him off cold turkey when I said it?"

"I don't know." Kelli shrugged. "I just really felt like I needed him at the time. Then after Daddy and I talked and prayed together, I slowly started seeing what you all had been trying to tell me. I talked with him a few times after that, but meeting with him just gave me an uncomfortable, guilty feeling from that point on."

"Well, whatever the motivation, I'm just glad you cut him off," Sasha said. "He'll just move on to the next girl, I'm sure. He's called a few times for you here at the store, but I told him you weren't in. A couple of them times I was lying, but a girl's got to do what a girl's got to do. If you never hear from him again, it'll still be two days too soon. Good riddance."

Kelli held her peace and walked into the storage room to check the inventory of children's Bibles. They'd been one of their best-selling items since the beginning of December. She didn't want to tell her friend that she too had been receiving constant calls from Stuart over the past few days.

After his second attempt to contact her, she'd set her cellular phone on vibrate so that no one would question as to why she wasn't answering calls. Anytime she saw his name on the caller ID, she'd let it forward into her voice mail. Plans were already set to have her number changed so that the calls would end.

Avoiding him in this manner seemed cowardly and insensitive on her part, but she had figured that by now he would have gotten the message and moved on. Seeing his number flash across her display screen an hour ago was a reminder to her that he'd not yet gotten the hint. He'd get it soon enough.

"Kelli!" She heard the loud whispering of her name and walked around the shelf to face Sasha.

"Who's watching the counter, Sasha?" Kelli asked. "What's wrong?"

"I never should have said his name," Sasha replied. "He must have heard me, because he's here."

"Who?"

"Stuart," she answered. "If the store had been empty, I would have given him a piece of my mind and sent him packing, but we have two other customers right now. You need to put this to rest once and for all, Kelli. This man is not getting the message. He's all cracked up. You can't treat him like he has good sense."

It was a talk that she didn't look forward to, but Kelli knew that the sooner she got this over with, the better. With a despondent sigh, she followed Sasha back into the store. Stuart stared at her without emotion as she walked to the counter and faced him. The grey shirt and paisley tie were the perfect accessories for the burgundy suit that he wore. The long grey wool overcoat was icing on the flawless cake. Although he *looked* good, Kelli knew that there was no place in her life for him.

"Hey," she said, seeing clearly the displeasure in his eyes.

"Is there some place that we can talk in private?" Stuart glanced toward Sasha as he posed the question.

The two browsing customers exited the store without purchasing anything, but in Sasha's opinion, their timing was perfect. She wouldn't have been able to hold back the words that pressed forward on her tongue in response to his suggestion.

"Unfortunately, this is a *public* business," Sasha interrupted. "Unlike your private practice, we don't have any secluded offices where people can meet and talk in secret. So, I guess you'll just have to talk to her right here."

"I wasn't speaking to you," Stuart shot back.

"Stop it. Both of you," Kelli said. "We really don't have any private rooms, Stuart," she said, "but that's okay. I already know why you're here."

"Do you?"

"Yes. I haven't returned your phone calls."

"And why is that?"

"I've decided to work on my marriage on my own," Kelli said.

"And you couldn't pick up the phone and tell me that?"

"I'm sorry," Kelli told him. "You're right. I should have done that. It's just that things are going well right now, and I've been focusing on keeping them that way. I apologize for not telling you how I felt."

"What do you mean, things are going well?"

"Jhordan and I had a heart-to-heart talk right before Christmas. He explained everything."

"He told you about the affair, and you're just going to let it slide?"

"He wasn't having an affair. You were right all along," she said. "When you said that it could be something else, you were right. It was. He was never having an affair."

"That's what he told you?" Stuart asked.

"Yes."

"And you believe him?"

"Stuart—"

"I can't believe you bought it. What reason did he give you for his behavior, Kelli?"

"That really ain't your business," Sasha broke in.

"I wasn't talking to you," Stuart snapped.

"Stop it!" Kelli ordered both of them. "I would think that you'd be happy for me," she told him. "He validated your point. It was a very long, painful, and personal story for Jhordan to tell me, Stuart. I don't want to go into it, but it explained everything."

"Let me explain *everything* to you," Stuart said as he suddenly reached forward and grabbed Kelli's arm. "Your husband is lying to you, Kelli. He's a liar and a cheater, and you need to stop letting him use you like this. He's making you look like a fool."

"Ouch! That hurts, Stuart."

"What Jhordan is going to do to you is going to hurt even more," he said. "He's not the one who cares about you, Kelli. *I'm* the one who cares about you. Don't you see that?"

"Let her go!" Sasha said as she delivered a punch, as hard as she could throw it, to his arm.

The sound of voices as more patrons entered the store brought the mounting altercation to a screeching halt. Kelli pulled her arm away when she felt Stuart's grip loosen. He seemed to struggle with regaining his composure. Straightening his coat, he took a deep breath, stood up tall, and backed away slightly.

"I'm sorry," he said softly.

"I think you should leave," Kelli said.

"And if you *ever* come back in this store," Sasha harshly whispered, "you're gonna be sorrier than that. I swear on my granddaddy's grave I'll have you locked up so fast it'll make your head spin."

Kelli's heart was pounding double time in her chest, and her knees felt weak with fear as she watched the exit door close behind him.

15

FLAME

Jhordan felt refreshed after stepping from the fire-house locker-room showers. It had been a busy day for the Biloxi Fire Department. A small three-passenger plane had crashed into an abandoned apartment build-ing, and the resulting blaze required a team effort from several neighboring stations.

No survivors meant pulling charred bodies from what was left of the wreckage. It was days like this one that turned his job from being heroic to being just plain grim. The deceased victims were a father, a mother, and their ten-year-old daughter. Even the hot water from the shower couldn't wash away the images. It was a horrible way to die.

"I thought you were working a double shift," Orlan-do Felts, a fellow firefighter, said as he watched Jhordan gather his things. "It's only 5:00."

"There was a mix-up in the schedule," Jhordan told

him. "They mistakenly scheduled both Ryan and me," he explained. "Ryan wants to stay, and I don't, so I'm outta here."

"Must be nice," his coworker said with a short laugh. "After that mess we had today, I wish I could go home and hug my family too. Guess I'll see you tomorrow."

"Try Monday," Jhordan said. "Later," he added as he laughed at his friend's bewildered expression.

The man had echoed his own earlier thoughts. The remains of the family who thought that they'd just take a leisurely afternoon flight could have easily been Jhordan's own. The woman could have been Kelli, and the child could have been Jazmin. He couldn't believe all the time he'd wasted running from love. Life was too short, but whatever time he had left, he'd spend it making up for nearly a year of ignoring his wife and sometimes even neglecting his daughter.

Getting off from work now was perfect timing. He'd been counting the days until he could be with his wife in every way, and he knew that the day had finally arrived. It would be at least another hour and a half before she'd make it home.

Jhordan pulled out his cell phone when he pulled into the lot of Edgewater Mall. Mary almost seemed to stifle laughter as she agreed to play babysitter for Jazmin. She didn't sound as though it was an imposition, so Jhordan shrugged off his suspicions and continued his shopping quest.

Bath & Body Works and Victoria's Secret were two stores he'd shied away from when Christmas shopping for fear that whatever he purchased from them would add to the sex appeal that seemed to come naturally for Kelli. Today he smiled an almost cunning smile as he found the perfect lingerie for his wife.

"Would you like this bagged or gift wrapped?" one of the clerks behind the counter asked him.

He thought to himself that it didn't matter, because either way, she'd have no need for it tonight.

"Gift wrapped, please."

"I just love when men take time to buy intimate things for the women they love," the clerk said to her coworker minutes later, as they both watched Jhordan leave the store with the wrapped gift tucked under his arm.

Vanilla candles were Kelli's favorite. Jhordan remembered her lighting them on their wedding night. Since then, he'd given her very little need for the romantic scents, but tonight she'd need larger ones that burned longer. A saleslady at Bath & Body Works helped him to quickly pick out candles and body lotions to match.

His next stop was Genie the Florist, where he bought six long-stemmed red roses. For the finishing touch, on his way back toward the mall exit, Jhordan ducked into Sweets from Heaven and bought smooth milk chocolates that seemed to melt on contact with the tongue.

The skies were already darkening when he pulled into the vacant spot in front of the empty apartment four doors down from theirs. In the unit to its immediate left lived a man who drove a delivery van. It was the perfect place in the back to hide his truck so that Kelli wouldn't see it upon her arrival.

Once inside their apartment, he began immediately setting the stage for a performance that his bride would never forget.

A strange feeling engulfed Kelli as she left her job to start her weekend. For the first time, she found herself looking over her shoulders as she walked to her car in the well-lit, near-empty parking lot. On her drive home, she periodically looked in her rear- and side-view mirrors. Stopping for gas, she constantly scoped her surroundings for any signs of being followed.

Stuart's behavior had frightened her. She understood him being disappointed at the way she decided to end the relationship with him, which she never should have started in the first place. It became clear, though, that what she thought was a healthy friendship, he'd begun seeing as something different.

Sasha had been right all along about Stuart's true intentions. Kelli had always hated it when she heard people refer to church girls who were brought up like her as naïve, but now she felt naïve. She couldn't believe that she never saw his attentiveness as sinister. Stuart's words today were the first he'd ever uttered that referenced Jhordan's disloyalty to her. Sharper still were his words that indicated that he—not Jhordan—was the one for her. How had she misread his intentions all this time?

She pulled into her complex and sat in the car for several moments before shutting off her engine. Just a few Sundays ago, Pastor Berry had preached a message about doing wrong and living in fear because of it. This must be what it felt like.

Kelli reached for the bag of goodies that she had bought to set the tone for her evening with Jhordan. Second-guessing her plans, she wondered if instead she should tell him about Stuart and how she'd confided in him when she was confused about their marriage. He wouldn't be home until near midnight, she thought, so she'd have plenty of time to decide what she would do and to rehearse the right words to say. The last thing she wanted was to spoil the plans she had because of something or someone as insignificant as Stuart and his foolish imaginations.

The bags in her hand, coupled with the thought that someone could still be following or watching her made her fumble with her keys as she struggled to unlock the door. When the door finally swung open, Kelli found herself temporarily paralyzed by the image before her eyes.

Glowing candles seemed to be everywhere. She eased the door shut behind her and placed her bags on the nearest sofa. As she looked toward the floor, she saw a single row of red rose petals that led from the front door toward the bedroom. The soft scent of vanilla filled the room.

The soulful, sultry sounds of Donny Hathaway's *A Song for You* got louder as she walked slowly towards the room where she'd slept alone for most of the past ten and a half months. Pushing the door open, she found more candles and Jhordan standing at the foot of the bed in a black and red silk robe holding a single rose in one hand and a wrapped gift in the other. He'd never looked so handsome.

She couldn't seem to take her eyes off of him as he walked toward her. Jhordan extended the items in his hand toward Kelli, but when she reached for them, he pulled them away and tossed them aside on the chair in the corner. Instead, he gently pulled her to him and swayed her body slowly to the music that played on the stereo.

Halfway through *I Love You More Than You'll Ever Know,* he had removed her clothes and was sending a mountain of chills through her body while his hand explored every curve of her frame. Kelli had untied the belt that held his robe together and slipped her hands inside. By the time the lyrics of *You Were Meant for Me* began, they'd finally made their way to the bed where their bodies intertwined rhythmically, taking them to heights of passion that they'd never experienced.

Afterward, still with no use for words, they lay quietly together. Kelli wiped a tear from her face as she lay with her head on Jhordan's chest. With one hand, he brushed his fingers through her hair. With the other, he stroked his fingers up and down the small of her back. With her ear pressed so close to his upper body, Kelli could hear and feel the pounding of his heart—beating quickly at first, but slowly returning to its normal pace. She felt the strokes of his hands slow and eventually come to a stop, and the change in his breathing pattern indicated that he'd drifted off to sleep.

"I love you," she whispered.

The music ended. Kelli stared at the candle that Jhordan had placed on the nightstand beside the bed. The flame on that one seemed higher than the other candles that burned in other areas of the room. It seemed to be symbolic of the new fire that had been kindled in their marriage.

She couldn't ruin it by telling Jhordan about Stuart McMillian. She and Sasha had made themselves quite clear during his unsolicited visit today. If there had been any question of where she stood before, she was sure that Stuart had gotten the message. While she'd valued the short-lived social contact that she thought she'd shared with him, Stuart's actions today made her realize that befriending him had been an act of bad judgment on her part.

Moving up gingerly on the bed so as not to wake her husband, she stared into his sleeping face for several moments before bringing her face to his and kissing his lips lightly. The sudden brief involuntary change in his breathing pattern both amused and flattered her. Wanting a repeat reaction, she kissed him again. This time as she pulled away, she was momentarily startled as she found herself looking into his opened eyes.

Reaching for her face, Jhordan pulled her back into him—pressing her lips to his, caressing her mouth more than kissing it. Then, without detaching his lips from hers, he turned his body and, with the strength of one arm, pulled Kelli beneath him. Without the music to guide them, they found a tempo that once again put their bodies in exquisite harmony with one another.

16

IN THE MEANTIME

The wind chilled Kelli's ears as she stepped from her car—but on the inside, she was basking in the afterglow. It was a romantic escapade that she wouldn't soon forget.

"Mommy!" Jazmin exclaimed when she spotted Kelli crossing the grass to meet them in the park near her parents' home.

"Hi, sweetie!" Kelli hugged her tightly. The choice the little girl had made on her own to refer to Kelli as her mother added a special flavor to the bond of their already close relationship.

"Hi, Mama," Kelli said when she reached the seated women. "Hey, Cheryl."

"Hey," both women said with grins that screamed, *We know what you've been doing!*

"Are we leaving now, Mommy?"

"We'll stay a little longer. Why don't you go back and play with the twins?" Kelli urged.

The three women sat in silence and watched the children play with the new toys they'd gotten for Christmas. Jazmin loved her role as the oldest playmate. Christopher and Tonya, bundled warmly in new coats and hoods, followed her every command as though they respected her as their trusted leader. The small neighborhood park was generally full of parents and their children on Sundays, but as the temperatures dropped, so did the attendance.

"So are you going to tell us about your weekend, or are we going to have to beat it out of you?" Cheryl spoke up.

Though the Jenkins women shared a definite love, most of it was unspoken. Kelli had never given details of her private life to her mother or her sister, and they had shared none with her either. Their relationship had never been on that level. She looked at her sister in surprise at the notion that she should reveal such intimate information.

"Why you looking at me like that?" Cheryl asked. "We're all adults here. Me and Mama know you and Jhordan weren't playing jacks for two and a half days."

"Not unless that's a new name for it these days," Mary mumbled with a chuckle.

"I ain't telling y'all what went on," Kelli said in embarrassment.

"Fine," Cheryl said. "Keep it to yourself then. We're not gonna beg you. We don't find your life *that* intriguing."

Quiet rested among them once more. Christopher's tearful cries broke the monotony of their watch and captured their attention. He'd fallen as he and his playmates chased one another round the swing set. Quickly vacating her seat, Cheryl rushed to assist Jazmin in checking him for bruises.

"Girl, I done kept your baby for two nights," Mary said in a low whisper to her youngest daughter. "You *owe* me."

"Mama!" Kelli said in shock.

"You know you want to tell us," Mary said with a wide grin. "Look at you. You 'bout to bust with excitement."

Kelli looked at her mother and smiled. She shook her head and turned away. Her mother was right—she did want to talk about her marriage's resurrection. The plan she'd made was to tell Sasha the whole story at work tomorrow, but now what had once seemed unnatural became normal.

"He was already home when I got in from work Friday evening," Kelli said just as her sister reclaimed her seat.

The three of them giggled like schoolgirls as Kelli told the edited, "G-rated" version of the activities that took place in the confines of her apartment on Friday night and all day Saturday.

"Umph," Cheryl said. "The last time Tony and I had an episode like that, we ended up with twins."

"No thanks," Kelli said as she shook her head vigorously. "I feel like I'm just getting to know Jhordan. For us, Jazmin will be it for a while."

"When was the last time you and Daddy had a weekend like that, Mama?"

Kelli's mouth dropped open. She couldn't believe what Cheryl had just said. She would never have even thought of posing such a question to their mother, and she braced herself for the scolding that she knew Cheryl was in for.

"Oh, it's been awhile," Mary said thoughtfully. "It's been 'bout a month now."

"A *month!*" Kelli couldn't decide whether she was more shocked at her mother's answer or by the fact that her mother had actually given an answer.

"What?" Mary said while peering over her sunglasses. "You think just 'cause we're your parents mean we don't still enjoy each other? It's easy for young men like Tony and Jhordan to be all energized and vibrant. Now, if they can still do it thirty or thirty-five years from now—*then* we can talk."

"Are you trying to tell us that Daddy's 'Da Man,' Mama?" Cheryl asked.

"Turn to your neighbor and say 'Ooooweee!'" Mary said.

The sisters crumpled onto each other as they laughed at their mother's words and her mimicking of Pastor Berry's habit. Once they'd calmed themselves, they returned to silently watching the children playing just thirty feet away.

Kelli's mind drifted as her eyes followed Jazmin. It was amazing the joy that Jhordan's daughter had brought to her life. During the time of the greatest strain in their marriage, it was the knowledge that the little girl counted on and trusted Kelli that kept her holding on and praying for the best. Jhordan agreed that Jazmin had been a stabilizing factor that kept him sane after his divorce and during this difficult time with Kelli.

The sound of a car's horn turned the three women's heads toward the street. The tinted window of a Mercedes slid down.

"Can you ladies tell me where the Casino Magic Biloxi Hotel is?"

"Yes," Mary answered. "It's on Beach Boulevard."

"Thank you," the man said. "Pretty kids you got there," he mentioned with a smile just before driving away.

"Everybody wants to gamble on Beach Boulevard," Mary huffed. "The devil sho' know how to reel them in, don't he?"

Kelli didn't even realize that her mother was directing the comment and question toward her. Even with the chilly breeze blowing, she felt perspiration breaking through on her brow and running down the side of her face. All of her insides shook as though some type of electric shock was being administered to her from the inside out.

"Kelli?" Cheryl called her.

"Kelli, what's wrong with you?" Mary said.

She could hear their voices, but Kelli couldn't seem to respond. She felt faint, and her throat felt like she'd just swallowed a tablespoon of talcum powder.

"Kelli!" her mother whispered frantically, trying not to alarm the children who were still playing just a few feet away. "Kelli!" she said again as she delivered three pats to her daughter's cheek.

"I have to go," Kelli finally said, pools of water flooding her eyes. "I have to get Jazmin and go."

"Go where?" Cheryl asked. "What happened?"

"Oh, God help me!" Kelli buried her tearful face in her hands. "He's gonna hurt my baby."

"Who?" Mary asked.

"Him!" Kelli pointed toward the direction of the empty street that ran alongside the park.

"The man that just left?" Mary asked in confusion. "He ain't gonna hurt nobody. He just asked for directions."

"I know him. He lives right here in Biloxi. That's the

man I told you about that I had dinner with. His name is Stuart McMillian. He knows where Beach Boulevard is, and he knows what hotels are there. He's *following* me, and what he just said was a way of threatening Jazmin's safety."

"Here," Cheryl said as she fished a baby wipe from the toddler bag that she carried. "Wipe your face before Jazmin looks over here and sees you crying."

"Keep talking, Kelli," her mother urged.

Kelli experienced emotions ranging from anger to regret to embarrassment as she further shared the relationship that she'd established with Stuart over the past recent weeks. Even in hindsight, she didn't know what she'd said or done to make him believe that she had any emotional attachment to him.

"If you believe this man is following you and threatening your family," Cheryl said, "then you need to tell the police."

"I can't go to the police with unproven suspicions, Cheryl. What am I going to say? He stopped and asked us for directions when he knows where the place is? That's not going to fly with the police. *I* know that he was sending a message to me by doing that, but *they* aren't going to see it that way.

"His firm is McMillian At Law, a very powerful firm—especially in the black community. I won't have the upper hand if I go to the police right now. That's the sad part. I'd have to wait until he actually hurt me or Jazmin before they'd do anything."

Kelli told her mother and sister about her last threatening encounter with Stuart.

"You can tell them how he came to the store," Cheryl pointed out. "Sasha can be your witness that he came up there and threatened you."

"He didn't openly threaten me at the store, Cheryl. He grabbed my arm while he was talking, but nobody's going to see that as a threat."

"I'll tell you what," Mary finally said. "All that is fine and good. You probably right. The police ain't gonna do nothing at this point, but you better keep a watchful eye out. I don't know how in the world you let yourself get all tied up with some stranger that you ain't know a hill of beans about. When you first talked about this attorney over dinner a few weeks back and got all flip-mouthed with me, I knew the devil had his filthy hands in this somewhere."

"Mama—" Kelli started.

"Hush up, now," Mary warned. "I ain't fixing to get back in all of that. I'm just here to tell you that you done got in a situation here that now is involving more than just you. It may be too early for you to go to the police, but you can go to Jhordan and tell him about all this. He's got a right to know."

"Oh, help," Kelli sighed heavily.

"I know what you're thinking," her mother said. "You think that if you go to him and tell him about all this, it's gonna set you back again. Things been going good for y'all for the past week, and you don't want to chance messing it up."

"I *can't* mess it up, Mama. I finally have the marriage I've been praying for."

"If you can't be honest in your marriage, you ain't got no marriage," Mary told her. "That's what got your marriage in trouble in the first place, Kelli," she reminded her. "Jhordan was keeping stuff from you, and it just about tore your marriage apart. You want that to happen again?"

"Of course not, Mama, but . . ."

"Then put an end to it right now, Kelli. I know you ain't never particularly liked being told what to do, but if you take only one piece of advice that I've given you, take this one. I know that you thought your involvement with Mr. McMillian was harmless, but now you know it wasn't.

"That fool is riding around town, following and threatening you right in your mama's face. That right there tells me that an education and a degree don't necessarily mean you ain't a fool. Between me and your daddy, the good lawyer is liable to need a good doctor. You might not be able to go to the police right now, and you can't file no restraining orders or criminal reports, but you *can watch and pray*. In the meantime, you have a husband who adores you and a daughter who trusts you. That's where your attention needs to be right now. Talk to him, Kelli."

"I agree," Cheryl nodded.

"Kelli," Mary said when she noted the fearful hesitation in her daughter's eyes. "*Talk* to him."

17

Chocolate Thoughts

Jhordan sat at the long wooden table and stared at the breakfast in front of him. Maybe it was the sweet taste of the residue that he'd licked off of his fingers moments earlier —he wasn't sure, but something about the toasted brown dessert made him think of Kelli. How ironic, that the flavor of the pastry was called "chocolate thoughts."

Last night, she'd seemed a bit distant as they sat together and went over Jazmin's holiday study list that needed to be turned in in just a couple of days. Math had never been her strongest subject, but Jhordan was proud that Jazmin had put in extra study time, and of the twelve problems she had to solve, all but one were correct.

After sending their daughter off to bed, he had questioned Kelli concerning her quietness over the past two days. She told him that she was fine, and when she'd snuggled close to him and kissed his neck, his brief concerns had been shooed away and replaced by feelings far more enjoyable.

He and Kelli had lain awake in bed for hours and found creative ways to eat the candies that he had purchased days earlier for her at Sweets from Heaven. Even tastier was the way she had looked as she finally put on the lingerie he'd bought and she'd modeled teasingly for his pleasure. Remembering their evening of lovemaking and dessert-tasting sparked something inside of him.

"Greetings, my African brother."

Jhordan laughed and shook his head at the only man in the fire station that he considered a friend. It would be a waste of time to correct him. Orlando knew where Jhordan was from, but to him, any black person who spoke with an accent other than American came from Africa.

"Greetings," Jhordan responded.

"So, you're the one who got the last chocolate glazed donut," Orlando said, breaking Jhordan's thoughts as he sat next to him.

"Sorry," Jhordan said, wiping chocolate icing from his mouth. "You snooze, you lose."

"I guess so," his friend conceded, then took a bite of his own treat. "You never told me what you did when you took last weekend off," he said with his mouth still full. "You and the family go anywhere special?"

Jhordan fought the smile that tugged at his lips. He and Kelli had spent those days traveling to many places without ever leaving the house. He licked another deposit of chocolate from his finger and struggled to bring his mind back to the conversation at hand.

"Well, did you?" Orlando asked.

"No," Jhordan said. "I spent 90 percent of it in bed, actually."

"I heard that," Orlando said, without a clue of Jhordan's reference. "Ain't nothing like a few days to just rest. You know what I mean?"

"Yeah," Jhordan said, still stifling the satisfactory smile that wanted to break through.

The two of them, along with others who had sat to eat, finished their snacks and gathered their things before heading for the staff meeting that had been scheduled prior to the holidays but had never materialized. Orlando and the others who worked with Jhordan—the fire chief included—saw Jhordan as a different breed of fireman. His association with the New York Fire Department and his participation in saving lives in the infamous September 11 disaster made him a champion among champions.

Jhordan avoided conversations about that time in his life. The others thought that it was his way of being modest. None of them knew the pain that thoughts of New York still brought to him—pains that started before and went far beyond 9/11. Even now, though he felt tons lighter since sharing his secret hurts with his wife and her family, the excitement that the very mention of the Big Apple brought the people in this small southern state only made him want to vomit.

The meeting was short. The fire chief thanked them for their bravery for the year, passed out the tentative work schedule for the month of January, and dismissed them, telling them that they could take New Year's Eve leisurely unless an emergency arose.

When there were no fires to keep them busy, every day at work was a long one for Jhordan, but his thoughts and the building excitement of the days and weeks ahead made days like this one even longer. His father and sisters, all who still lived in Trinidad and Tobago, were about to meet his bride in a few short weeks for the first time.

Admittedly, remembrance of the circumstances surrounding his mother's death always made him hesitant about returning home, especially to the house where his father still lived. This time, though, he felt honored that he would be celebrating his first anniversary in his native land and around family.

Napoleon Adams disliked Sadonia from the day Jhordan took her to Trinidad to meet him a month before their wedding. She had complained about everything from the weather to the food, and her constant degradation of his homeland had been a slap to the face of Jhordan's father.

That was no worry with Jhordan this time around. He knew that his father and sisters would approve of Kelli. His present bride wouldn't have to win their hearts. They would fall in love with her as quickly and as easily as Jazmin had. Trinidad's Carnival would unveil an entirely different side of his life that he couldn't wait to show Kelli.

"You think you gonna get home tonight in time enough to kiss the wife before the clock strikes twelve?" Orlando's voice broke Jhordan's thoughts again as he took a seat in the chair across from him and began setting up the checkerboard. It was the game of choice of both men when they wanted to keep their minds off the slowly moving hands on the clock.

"I'm supposed to get off at eleven tonight," Jhordan said while grabbing the black chips and setting them up in the appropriate squares. "I didn't think kissing me before midnight was a big deal, but Kelli did mention wanting to do it. So, even if for some reason the traffic is bad, I'll get there in time to make her wish come true."

"I get off at eleven too," Orlando said. "I've gotten a midnight kiss every year for the last six years, but since

164

me and Tracey broke up I ain't got nobody to kiss this year."

"Yeah, I can relate, man. I've definitely had some lonely New Year's Eves."

The minutes and hours passed slowly on the clock on the wall. Kelli and Jazmin had taken down the Christmas decorations, played a game of Go Fish, baked cookies, read three books together, and shared a bag of fresh popcorn. It was finally only a few minutes before 11:00, and Jazmin had given up on her fight to stay awake until her daddy got home.

Kelli sat on the floor near the sofa where Jazmin slept and wrote in the pages of her journal while she waited for her husband's arrival. The traditional kiss before the New Year had never had any meaning to her before now. She didn't believe in bad luck, so fearing the results of not kissing someone had never been a problem.

Her desire to kiss Jhordan had nothing to do with luck at all. She wanted to kiss him because she loved her husband's full lips and the skillful ways he used them. It wasn't just about what was customary in the States; Kelli wanted their New Year's kiss to symbolize the newness of their passions and to be a seal for all the years to come. Any excuse to kiss Jhordan was reason enough.

As she looked back on the recent days of her journal notes, she'd almost been writing in code. Her worries were hidden between the words on the pages, but they resurfaced as she reread them. When she wrote of her desire to hold Jazmin close and love her forever, it was really a fear that something was about to happen to take her away. Her written wishes that Jhordan and she could fly so high into the heavens that only God would know their whereabouts was her way of saying that she wanted to feel safe from the man she had once trusted but now feared.

After closing her diary, she immediately checked the locks on the doors and made sure that her home security alarm was set. Kelli always felt so much more protected when Jhordan was at home. Whatever fears she experienced in his absence were rarely even considered when he was there with her.

At 11:15 the telephone rang. On the caller ID was the number to the firehouse. She thought that Jhordan would be on his way home by now. It was at least a half-hour drive. If he didn't hurry, he'd be pressed for time.

"Hello," she answered.

"Hey, baby," Jhordan said.

"What's wrong?" Kelli asked. "Why are you still at work? Is there a fire?"

"No," he said. "A fire would make sense. We can't make sense of this, though."

"What?"

"I think somebody got Halloween mixed up with New Year's Eve," Jhordan said. "Some prankster went through our parking lot and punctured James Addison's tires and mine. We're trying to figure out why. The only thing we can think of is that both of our cars are the latest ones in the lot."

"Oh, no!" Kelli's heart pounded. She couldn't prove it, but she knew Stuart was behind it in some way. "Oh, no," she repeated.

"It's okay, baby," Jhordan said, tring to calm her. "I just wanted you to know that I wouldn't be home in time for our kiss. We gotta try to see if we can get somebody to open shop long enough for us to get some wheels. One of the guys here knows the owners of Goodyear on this side of town. You'll be okay until I can get home, won't you?" Jhordan asked. "I promise I'll make it up to you."

"I'll be okay," Kelli said, trying not to sound panicky as she spoke.

"I love you."

"I love you too," she said.

Hanging up the phone, she tried to slow her heartbeat by taking deep breaths and speaking reassuring words to herself while she paced the carpet. It didn't work. She was unable to fool herself into thinking that this was not the work of Stuart McMillian. Kelli couldn't believe how stupid she had been. During those cry-on-the-shoulder moments that she'd spent with Stuart, she'd shared so much of her personal life that she shouldn't have. Not once did she consider that it would come back to haunt her.

Kelli remembered telling Stuart where Jhordan worked and that he drove a black truck. When she had first met Stuart at the restaurant where she and Jhordan frequented, she had stressed the point of needing to be careful. Stuart must've vandalized both vehicles because of the vanity plates with the initials JA. Both Jhordan and his coworker had the same initials. It was him all right. Kelli was sure of it.

She sighed as she paced the floor and tried to remember what else she may have told him. It was totally her fault that he knew the neighborhood that her parents lived in. He'd told her about the neighborhood he'd grown up in near Decatur, Georgia, a suburb of Atlanta, and she'd responded by telling him where she'd been raised. It had appeared to be harmless chatter at the time, but now it seemed that she'd put her own husband in harm's way. Not only was Stuart terrorizing and possibly stalking her, but indiscreetly he was doing the same to the people she loved the most. More recollections of her conversation with Stuart were coming back to her. She was even more convinced that he'd been the one to cripple the vehicles.

Had she told him where she lived? Kelli thought hard. She was almost certain that she hadn't, but she couldn't remember. Kelli looked at the clock on the wall. It was 11:25 p.m.

"Wake up, Jazmin," she called as she shook the girl.

Jazmin sat up slowly and rubbed her eyes. "Is Daddy here?" she asked.

"No, sweetie." Kelli fought to disguise her fright. "We're going to get him. Come on."

Grabbing her purse and keys, she and Jazmin hurried from the apartment, and Kelli quickly locked the doors once they were inside the car. It was 11:27. She had to get to Jhordan. They'd be safe there. Not only that, but she was determined not to let Stuart and his tactics steal away the kiss that she'd earmarked as the one to seal the passion in her marriage.

Thirty-one minutes later, she was pulling into the parking lot of the fire station. Dark, unfamiliar shadows of the men and women who worked there swarmed the lot as they stood around discussing what had taken place earlier that evening.

"I'm Kelli Adams," Kelli said to a woman who was standing near the entrance door. "Can you tell me where my husband, Jhordan, is?"

"He's inside," she said. "I think he just went in to call you."

"Thank you." Kelli walked inside, holding tightly to Jazmin's hand.

"Hey, Daddy," Jazmin called. She'd spotted him

first, standing by the telephone chatting with Orlando as he dialed.

"Hey, pumpkin," he said after the initial surprise of seeing them. "What are you all doing here?"

Kelli outran Jazmin to his arms. The few employees that were inside looked on in admiration and amusement as Kelli reached up and pulled Jhordan's lips to hers. From a television in the distance, she could hear the end of the countdown and then the cheers from the people standing in Times Square who had gathered to watch the New Year's Eve ball drop.

"Happy New Year," she whispered as she released him.

18

BABY MOMMA DRAMA

With temperatures well into the forties on the outside and a repaired heating and cooling system on the inside, Biloxi Temple was a much more comfortable place to be in amid the bright lights of the cameras in the first videotaped service of the New Year.

Packed nearly to capacity, the church structure seemed to shake as the choir sang an upbeat interactive song that brought the congregation to its feet. Kelli smiled up at Jhordan who stood beside her with Jazmin perched in his arms as though she were still a toddler. It was his answer to the child's earlier complaint of not being able to see when everyone stood.

Kelli could feel her mother's eyes burning into the side of her face from clear across the adjacent aisle. In a lengthy telephone conversation with her mother last night, Mary pleaded with Kelli to tell Jhordan about her past involvement with Stuart.

"The mere fact that you ain't told him is gonna make him suspicious of just how far you went with this man," her mother had told her.

"Mama, I told you—"

"I know what you told me, Kelli," she had interrupted. "I know you said that nothing happened between the two of you, and I believe you. I'm just telling you what Jhordan is going to think. It would be different if Stuart had accepted the fact that you no longer want to deal with him, but he hasn't. He's pestering you, and now he done went and messed up Jhordan's truck. What are you waiting for? You gonna let something too terrible to imagine happen before you tell him? You gonna let him hurt Jaz—"

"Don't say it, Mama!" Kelli had been near tears.

"Kelli, this ain't about just you anymore," Mary had told her. "It stopped being just a Kelli problem a long time ago. If you were the only one being affected by all of this, you could see it as only your personal problem and deal with it in your own way. But you're not the only one being affected, and you can't sit back and do nothing."

"Mama, not only have I not seen Stuart, but I haven't heard a word from him since the New Year's Eve incident. It's a good sign. I've really been praying hard, and God has finally answered my prayers. There's no need for me to stir up unnecessary trouble between Jhordan and me. It's over," Kelli had said in as convincing a tone as she could. "Stuart isn't a problem for me or anyone else anymore."

"I got a flooded front yard that's calling you a liar right now," Mary had said.

"What?"

"That's right," she had said. "Me and Wesley woke up this morning, and the spigot that's attached to the front of the house that we use for watering the lawn was

172

turned on full speed. The whole front yard was flooded, and water was even gathered out on the sidewalk and the edge of the street."

"What?" Kelli had repeated in shock.

"I know me and your daddy raised you to be smarter than this, Kelli. Yes, we taught you to believe in God and in the power of prayer, but we ain't never taught you to use God as an excuse for not owning up to your mistakes. This whole mess is going to come to the surface one way or the other. This man might be a lawyer, but he needs to be locked up. You can't just pray this one away, baby. You got to talk to Jhordan so that y'all can work together on bringing this to a peaceful end."

Before she had hung up the phone, Kelli had promised her mother that she'd speak to Jhordan. When he had walked into the house, though, and praised her for making her spaghetti with his favorite sauce, she couldn't bring herself to do it. Kelli hadn't spoken with her mother since, but she knew that her mother sensed that no discussion on the matter had taken place since their conversation.

Pastor Berry's message hit home as though he had somehow been briefed on what was going on. The sermon on pleasing God by being faithful in everyday living brought "amens" from every corner of the church.

"Turn to your neighbor and say, 'How can I please God, who I've never seen, if I can't be truthful to you, who I see every day?'" Pastor Berry said.

Jhordan turned to her, but Kelli couldn't look back at him. With his index finger and thumb, he lifted her chin and turned her face to look in his direction. Instantly, Kelli could see in his eyes that he knew something was wrong. A tear trickled down her right cheek.

Quietly, he withdrew his hand and returned his focus to the pages of the Bible in front of him.

From the corner of her eye, Kelli saw him slowly shake his head in disbelief. She read his thoughts loud and clear. *I knew it. I knew I couldn't trust her. I knew this was too good to be true!*

The closing prayer had barely ended and Kelli had hardly had a chance to put on her coat when Jhordan sent Jazmin to play with the twins. Kelli's eyes briefly met her mother's before Jhordan slipped his hand into hers and pulled her in the direction to follow him. Mary's eyes were sympathetic. They didn't have the "I told you so" look that Kelli was familiar with from the past. Still, her mother had warned her, and now she had to face the music.

For several moments, they stood in silence—facing each other beside their car door in the church's parking lot. Jhordan seemed apprehensive about asking any questions in fear of what answers he might receive.

Not able to find the right words to say, Kelli burst into tears. "He was only a friend," she blurted.

"Oh, please," Jhordan whispered. It was worse than he thought. He turned and began walking away.

"Baby, wait," Kelli said, running to him and catching him by the arm. "It's not like that. It's not what you think."

"You're seeing someone else?" Jhordan's eyes were filled with hurt and unmitigated disbelief. "Another man?"

"No," she said as she buried her face in his chest. "Please don't walk away. Please listen to me. Please," she begged.

Jhordan pulled her away from him and released a lung full of air that caused his cheeks to expand. Rubbing his hands over his freshly cut hair, he struggled with too many emotions to identify.

"I'm listening," he finally whispered.

"When we were having marital problems—Jhordan, wait," she said, stopping him again as he turned to walk away. "Please," she said again. "Please listen."

"Tell me you didn't have an affair." His voice trembled as he spoke. "I need to hear that right now," he said.

"I didn't have an affair, Jhordan," she quickly said. "I didn't. I promise."

Her assuring words seemed to bring some comfort. Jhordan leaned his back against the car beside her and stared straight ahead. "I'm listening," he repeated.

Kelli stepped away from the door of the car and stood in front of him. She wiped the existing tears from her face but felt new ones pooling in the corners of her eyes.

"When we were having problems," she began again, "I befriended this lawyer who shopped at the bookstore. On those evenings that you'd come home from work but would leave and stay out all night, I would call him, because I needed someone to talk to. A couple of times when you took Jazmin with you or when she was spending the night away from home, I met him for dinner, and he'd listen to me and tell me that everything was going to work out fine. When I'd tell him that I thought you were having an affair, he'd tell me not to think the worst. He said that maybe you were just going through something, and it would pass.

"The whole time, Jhordan, he never said one bad thing about you. He was always saying things that made me think he wanted us to work everything out. I thought he was my friend, but when I told him that I no longer needed him as my advisor, he turned into a different person."

"What do you mean he turned into a different person?"

"He stopped by the store one day, and he was angry that I wouldn't answer or return his phone calls. He told me that you were lying and that I should just face the fact that you were, in fact, having an affair. He said he was the one for me and not you."

"So, he wants you—is that what you're telling me?" Jhordan asked. "You flirted with some guy, and now he wants more."

"I wasn't flirting. I was just talking to him."

"So is this the *real* reason you changed your cell phone number? You told me that you just wanted to change it so that the last four digits spelled 'rack' like the name of your store, but *this* is really why you changed it, isn't it? He was calling you, wasn't he?"

Kelli nodded silently while wiping water from her face and chin. Jhordan blew out another puff of air, causing vapor to fly from his lips in the cold temperatures.

"When was the last time you saw him?" he asked.

"I haven't actually *seen* him since right after Christmas, but —"

"We reconciled before Christmas," Jhordan pointed out. "Why were you still seeing him?"

"I didn't see him socially—just when he came to the store. Since I told him I couldn't see him anymore, he's been acting out and doing things to upset my family."

"Like what?"

"He flooded my parents' front yard while they slept on Friday night," she began. "I can't prove it, but I know that he's the one who flattened your tires at work that night."

"What?"

"And one time he . . . he," she stammered, "he sort of hinted a threat toward Jazmin."

176

"He threatened Jazmin?" Jhordan's voice was at a whisper, but every word he said was saturated with fury. "He threatened my daughter, and you're just now telling me?"

"I thought it was over until I talked to Mama last night."

"A man you brought into our lives is now stalking you, your parents, Jazmin, and me, and you never once mentioned it? Are you being honest with me, Kelli? Are you sure you never had any other involvement with him?"

"Mama!"

Kelli quickly wiped the residue of tears from her face when she heard Jazmin's calls. She didn't need for her to find out that she and Jhordan had been having this emotional discussion. Quickly pulling her shades from her coat pocket, she slipped them on and turned toward Jazmin's call. To both of their surprise, Jazmin was running in the opposite direction and had jumped into the arms of another woman who was crossing the front lawn of the church.

"Great!" Jhordan sputtered softly in heightened exasperation. "What next?"

Even without him saying so, Kelli knew who the woman was. Jazmin was now pointing in their direction, and her mother was walking toward them while planting numerous kisses on Jazmin's cheek in the process.

In Kelli's eyes, Sadonia looked like a runway model. Her legs seemed to go on for miles beneath the leopard print dress, coat, and matching hat that she wore. In the distance, near the church entrance doors, Kelli saw her family standing together, looking on inquisitively.

"I don't need this," Jhordan whispered as though talking to himself. "Not now—I don't need this."

"I'm sorry." Kelli spoke softly as she looked at him through her dark glasses.

When the woman reached the place where they had been standing for the past several minutes, she lowered Jazmin to the ground and smiled as she looked at her ex-husband.

"Hi, Jhordan," she spoke. "How are you?" She was indeed a native New Yorker. Her voice carried no Southern distinction.

"What are you doing here?"

"A return greeting would have been nice," she said politely.

"I'm in no frame of mind for this, Sadonia." Jhordan battled to remain poised in front of his daughter. "What are you doing here?"

"Well, I just got here, so I can't be the source of your bad mood," she said. "You must be the present Mrs. Adams," she said sarcastically—finally acknowledging Kelli's presence.

Her tone brought a boil to Kelli's stomach. The fact that Sadonia had guessed right in suggesting that Kelli must have been the reason for Jhordan's attitude didn't make her feel any less insulted. Not sure what to say, Kelli remained quiet.

"Why are you here, Sadonia?" Jhordan asked for the third time.

"I had a couple of days off and thought I'd fly in to see . . ." She hesitated for a moment and then looked down at Jazmin. "My baby," she concluded.

"Jazmin, go to your grandparents," Jhordan told her.

"Am I going to go home with you and Mommy?" the girl asked. "Or do you want me to ride with them?"

Through her dark shades, Kelli saw Sadonia's eyes

squint in displeasure at the sound of hearing Jazmin's reference to her stepmother.

"Mommy's coming with you," Jhordan told her. Kelli looked up at Jhordan. She didn't want to leave. She wanted to stand by his side to find out Sadonia's true reasons for her visit. She wanted to hear every single word the woman had to say. However, Jhordan's total avoidance of eye contact with her combined with the trauma that she'd just caused him was all the encouragement she needed to take Jazmin's hand and lead her back across the lawn.

"I can't believe you did that," Sadonia said. "I only wanted to spend a little quality time with my daughter. Is that too much to ask?"

"That request was denied when you called and made it weeks ago," Jhordan said. "I can't believe you blatantly disregarded what I said and showed up here."

"I came a long way, Jhordan."

"That's neither Jazmin's problem nor mine," Jhordan said. "Jazmin isn't some rag doll that you can play with when you want to and throw away when you don't."

"Okay," Sadonia said, softening her tone, "maybe my past actions deserved that. I'm sorry. I got lonely in that big condominium all by myself. I had some days off, and I just wanted to spend it with her."

"When you *weren't* in that big condominium all alone, you didn't want her there. What's the matter? Have you worked your way all around New York now? Are there no men left for you to play house with?"

"Are you ever going to forgive me, Jhordan?" The tears that formed in her eyes were a result of pure nostalgia. "How many times do I have to apologize for what I did to you? I'm sorry that I hurt you and walked away from you. For years I've been trying to make it right, and you won't let me."

"It's not that I won't *let* you make it right—you *can't* make it right. I pray on a daily basis for you, Sadonia. You don't ever have to apologize to me. I've told you that before. I've moved on, but despite that, I don't want to see you. Your coming here doesn't make situations any better; it makes them worse."

"I know you don't believe this, Jhordan," Sadonia said as she took a single step toward him and lowered her voice as though concerned that someone might overhear, "but I've never stopped loving you."

"Stop it," Jhordan said through clinched teeth.

"And I've never stopped regretting the day that I had Pete's baby or the day I forced Jazmin from your arms and walked out—"

"Stop it!" he whispered abrasively. "That part of my life is over. I have a whole new life now."

"With her?" Sadonia asked. "I sat in my car for several minutes and watched the two of you arguing over here. You're not happy with her, Jhordan. She's just a—"

"Watch yourself," Jhordan warned.

"She can't do for you what I can do." Sadonia rephrased her sentence. "Remember how good we were together? Remember Hawaii? Yes, I messed it up," she said, "but I didn't understand what I had with you. I know how to do it for you. I know how to make you happy, Jhordan."

"The only thing you can do for me," Jhordan said slowly, "is to get on the first plane back to New York and never set foot near me again. If there is any chance of you doing anything to make me happy, that would be it."

Jhordan paused momentarily to allow two passing

church members to walk by them and out of listening range. Once they were a distance away, he continued.

"I want you to continue to be a part of Jazmin's life, Sadonia—but not at this price. I won't let you hurt or confuse her any more than you already have, and I won't let you manipulate your way into the affairs of my marriage. Yes, like any other married couple, Kelli and I have our differences. But make no mistake—I love her very much, and when I married her, I promised her and her parents that she wouldn't have to deal with any 'baby momma drama' and I intend to keep that promise.

"Now, I want you back on a plane that will land you at LaGuardia Airport *today*. And if I see you again without a mutual agreement on our parts, we will go back to the arrangement that *you* initially set when you signed Jazmin over to me. Take a good long look at her now," Jhordan said, pointing in the child's direction, "because I promise you, if you try me again, this is the last time you'll see her. Are we clear?"

19

No Regrets

The sounds of an array of music from instrumentals to rock to R&B classics played softly from the speakers at Edgewater Mall. Kelli sat at a table in the food court just outside of Chick-Fil-A and looked at her watch for the umpteenth time. If Jhordan were going to show up, he would have been there twenty minutes ago.

She'd slipped the invitation to meet her in with the lunch she'd packed for him that morning before she left for work. Her hope was that when he got ready to break for lunch, he'd see the note and make the drive to meet her instead of eating what she'd prepared. What she hadn't considered until now was that he may not even have taken the lunch with him when he left—or maybe he just didn't want to talk to her. She could certainly understand.

For the past two weeks, her home had been quieter than it had been since she and Jhordan had the talk that brought renewed strength and excitement to their marriage. Even Jazmin had become somewhat withdrawn and wasn't her usual bubbly self. Though she was young, she sensed what was going on between her father and Kelli.

Two nights ago, as Kelli checked through Jazmin's homework before putting the girl to bed, she had come across a colorful photo that she had drawn in her art class. The teacher had given her an excellent mark on the paper, but unlike in times past, Jazmin hadn't even shown the work to her parents. Kelli had questioned her as to why.

"I don't know." Jazmin had shrugged.

"It's beautiful," Kelli had said, hoping to lift the child's spirits.

"Do you know what it is?" Jazmin had asked as she sat on the bed beside her stepmother. Kelli's words had seemed to cheer her up just a bit. She had held up the colorful drawing for her to get a better view. Kelli had looked at it thoughtfully for a moment. By far, Jazmin wasn't the best artist in the world, but the figures had seemed legible enough to take a good guess at it.

"Let's see," Kelli had said. "That's two ladies swimming, and they're trying to get that little girl and her cat to join them in the swimming pool."

"No!" Jazmin had doubled with laughter.

"No?" Kelli had taken a closer look. It still looked the same. "What is it?"

"It's not two ladies," Jazmin had pointed out. "It's a man and a lady, and it's not a pool. It's you and Daddy swimming in the lake by Old Man Carlos' house. And it's not a cat. It's a dog. It's me and Papa's dog, Mutton," she had explained. "And we're not going to get in the water. We're just watching you and Daddy swim."

Sitting at the table sipping on a large cup of diet lemonade that she'd bought just so she wouldn't look out of place while taking up a table for two in the food court, Kelli's thoughts continued.

"Why'd you draw a picture of me and your daddy swimming in the lake?" she'd asked Jazmin.

"Because Mr. Baines told us to draw a picture of ourselves with our favorite people at a place where we would like to go and visit. I knew we were supposed to go to see Papa and to Aunt Jeanette's wedding, so that's what I drew—our trip to Trinidad. I figured that while we were there, we could swim in Old Man Carlos' lake. I guess we won't be doing that now."

Having said that, Jazmin seemed not to want to talk about it anymore as she tucked her feet under the covers of her bed and laid back on her pillow. Tears had clouded Kelli's vision at the sadness that Jazmin's tone carried. It had been clear to her that Jhordan's and her attempts to hide the friction between them had failed.

"Can I have it?" Kelli had asked as she stood at the door after turning out the light.

"Uh-huh," Jazmin had responded, looking at her through the darkness.

Wiping her mouth with her napkin, Kelli picked up the satchel that she'd placed by her feet and pulled out the drawing out that she'd been carrying around for two days. The colors that Jazmin had used to design the artwork spoke volumes of how happy she'd been when she'd created it, but the unhappiness she'd displayed when giving it to her was the image seared in Kelli's mind. She refolded the paper and prepared to gather her belongings.

"Greetings."

The sight of Jhordan's towering figure startled her, but it was the fact that he showed up at all that caused her heart to beat more rapidly. He was dressed in brown from head to toe—his jacket, turtleneck sweater, corduroy pants, and shoes. He looked like a tall order of chocolate pudding. At that moment, Kelli's stomach rumbled as though telling her that her fast from this appetizing dish had gone on far too long.

"You're leaving?" he asked her.

"No," Kelli said while easing her bag back onto the floor. "Please, sit down."

She watched intently as Jhordan removed his jacket and hung it on the back of his chair before occupying the chair directly across from her at the small table.

"Have you eaten?" she asked. "I can order you something."

"I'm not hungry," Jhordan answered, looking directly in her eyes.

"You look good," they said in unison, bringing a tension-breaking smile to both their faces.

"You wanted to talk," Jhordan said as he quickly sobered.

"Who's Old Man Carlos?" she asked.

"What?"

"Old Man Carlos," Kelli repeated. "Who is he?"

"Carlos Ramen lives on the property next to my father," Jhordan answered curiously. "When we were children, his wife would make clothes for my sisters—especially after my mother's death. Though Carlos is considerably older than my father, they used to work together building steelpans. Ms. Mariah, Carlos' wife, died nearly ten years ago. Old Man Carlos is a nickname given to him because he's somewhere in the neighborhood of eighty-five now."

Kelli had almost become engrossed in Jhordan's story. In her mind, she had pictures of Jhordan's father and the older man building the pans that Jhordan had just spoken of. She tried to imagine Jhordan as a small child, watching his older sisters parade proudly in the new clothes that they'd been given.

"Why do you ask?" he said, interrupting her thoughts.

Quietly, Kelli pulled the folded drawing from her satchel once more and opened it on the table in front of her husband.

"Jazmin drew this picture at school a few days ago," she said. "Her teacher put a big red A and drew a bright yellow smiley face on it, and she didn't even show it to us."

Jhordan stared at the paper in front of him and then picked it up to examine it closer. "This is nice," he remarked.

"It's *us*, Jhordan," Kelli told him. "The little girl is Jazmin, and that's the two of us swimming in the lake by Old Man Carlos' house. The teacher asked her to draw a picture of what she wanted to do with the people she loved, and that's what she drew. She didn't show it to us because she knows that there's a problem with us. She thinks her dream is ruined now, so she saw no need of sharing it with us."

"I never cancelled the trip home," Jhordan said.

"She's seven, Jhordan. In her mind, she believes that even if we go to your home, we won't be able to do *this*," Kelli said as she pointed at the paper.

"I didn't create *this*, Kelli."

"I know," Kelli whispered as she reached across the table to touch his hand. "I created this, and I'm not trying to deny that. Creating it was easy. I did it all by myself, but I need your help in order to make it go away."

"You brought another man into our marriage," Jhordan said.

"Please stop saying it like that," Kelli said. "That makes it sound like something that it wasn't."

"Kelli—"

"I was wrong, Jhordan," she interrupted him. "I'm not trying to downplay what I did. I never should have sought solace in Stuart, and I'm sorry. But *nothing* happened. All I ever did was talk to him; all I ever wanted to do was talk to him. You have to believe that. I had no idea that he would turn around and do the stupid things that he did when I told him that I no longer needed his support."

"For the first time in my life, I worry about Jazmin's welfare at school and your safety at the store," Jhordan said. "Do you know how hard it is to do my job under those circumstances and conditions? Your bad judgment has affected every person in our family."

"I'm sorry, Jhordan."

"Have you heard from him again?"

"No."

"Would you tell me if you had?"

"See, that's the worst part of all of this," Kelli said. "You don't trust a word I say anymore. That hurts me, Jhordan. Every time I answer you, you question my answer."

"You know what hurts me?" Jhordan challenged, leaning in close as he spoke just above a whisper. "You know what feels the worst about this to me? The fact that you chose *him*, that's what. When we got married, your mother took me aside and told me that she had nothing against me personally, but she said that you changed your whole plan for your future when you accepted my proposal, and that troubled her."

"What?" It was a conversation Kelli had never heard about.

"She told me that you'd always had big dreams of

marrying a man who was well educated and had a certain amount of influence and clout. She said that you were destined to marry a politician or an executive of some type. You'd always said that the reason you were waiting until you finished college to settle down and get married was because you felt it was only right to be able to offer your husband the same qualifications that you expected from him.

"Your Mr. Right was a man who sat behind a desk in corporate America—not a blue-collar brotha' who slid down a pole as a public servant in a firehouse," Jhordan said. "You wanted a husband who carried business cards and a briefcase, Kelli. Not a man who lugged around air tanks and water hoses.

"When the going got tough, you ran straight into the arms of a suit-wearing, moneymaking, corner-office professional. Don't you see what I see?" he asked her. "Even if nothing happened between the two of you, this lawyer is everything you ever said that you wanted in a man, and he was a magnet for you when you felt trapped. I can't compete with that, Kelli. I'll *never* be able to compete with that. If at the end of the day, his kind is what you really want—"

"He's *not,*" Kelli said as she reached forward and touched Jhordan's cheek. "I want nothing more at this moment than to be angry at Mama for telling you that," she said, "but I can't be. None of it is a lie. I said all those things, and I meant them at the time that I said them. But people change, Jhordan, and *I've* changed.

"When I met you, none of that other shallow stuff even mattered anymore. In my years of being single, I met plenty of men who wore suits, carried briefcases, and pulled in big money. If that was all I wanted, then I could have had that long before I met you. When I met you, *you* were all that mattered. I fell in love with a firefighter, and I couldn't be prouder of what you do if you were the president of the United States.

"I didn't change the things I wanted when I met you," she said; "*the things I wanted* changed when I met you. Even when you were never at home and I thought there was another woman in your life, my love for you never changed, Jhordan. I'd go through all of that confusion again if in the end we'd be sitting here right now, in the middle of the food court with people staring and all.

"I know that what I did put us all in an awful place, and I'm sorry. But the fact is I can't change the bad choice that I made to trust Stuart's shoulders as a safe place to cry. But I've made some good choices too, and giving my heart to you was one of them. I have absolutely no regrets in choosing you. The life you've given me as your wife and the mother of your daughter far outweighs whatever life I may or may not have had with anyone else."

Jhordan's eyes seemed to burn into her soul as he watched her from across the table. Kelli's hands caressed his on top of the table, and though his eyes were no longer filled with the angry betrayal that she knew had once overwhelmed him, Kelli found it hard to read his thoughts through his quiet gaze.

"Come on," he said after taking a glance at his watch. "I have to get back to work."

Once outside, Jhordan walked her to her car and unlocked the doors. "I'll see you at home later," he said.

"Jhordan," Kelli said as he kissed her forehead and began backing away. "I know that what I did wasn't the same as when you kept the secrets of your hurt from me, but the common denominator is that we both were wrong. You asked me to forgive you, and I did. Can't you forgive me too?"

"No regrets that I don't carry a briefcase?" Jhordan suddenly asked after a momentary silence.

"Baby, carrying little sissified briefcases don't build this kind of body," Kelli said, running her hand up the suede-covered sleeves of his jacket.

On the outside, though, all she could see was the pearly white teeth that broke from behind his lips. It was the warmest smile she'd seen him display in two weeks. He turned serious quickly, though, and cupped her face in his hands, forcing her to look into his eyes.

"I'm gonna be honest with you, Kelli," he told her. "My mind is telling me to run like the wind, but my heart won't let me. My heart says that you are the only woman in the world who would be still standing with me after what I put you through in our first year of marriage.

"With anyone else, I never would have been able to look forward to a first-year anniversary. My mind says to fear you for what may happen tomorrow. My heart says to love you as though there *is* no tomorrow."

"Listen to your heart," Kelli said, readily accepting the lips that he offered. His arms felt wonderful as he wrapped them around her body and held her closely to him. The winter temperatures were no match for the heat that she could feel building up inside of him.

"Come straight home after work," Jhordan whispered upon releasing her. With an unmistakable look of longing in his eyes, he turned and walked away.

20

EMOTIONS

All seemed still and quiet. Every day Kelli prayed that Stuart had become bored with his own mind games and had moved on. She felt confident in her prayers, but she was reminded of what her faulty judgment had caused when Jhordan began personally taking Jazmin to school to ensure her safe arrival.

With no concrete proof or eyewitnesses to verify her family's theory, there was nothing to prove Stuart's guilt. Jhordan, Tony, and Wesley went together as a unit to pay a visit to the chief of police at the Biloxi Police Department, but due to lack of evidence, nothing could be done. All of them had now established a daily chain of events that would allow each of them to know that they were safe at all times. Kelli felt that it was unnecessary, but her father had insisted.

When Kelli got to work each morning, she'd have to call Jhordan to let him know that she had arrived safely.

When Jhordan got to work, he'd have to call Kelli and let her know the same. Upon picking Jazmin up from school, Wesley or Mary would call Jhordan to inform him that everything was all right.

Once Jazmin had completed her homework after school, she and the twins were not allowed to play outside without the constant supervision of one or both of their grandparents. If any of them, Tony and Cheryl included, saw anything or anyone that looked suspicious, they were to contact Jhordan and Kelli and, if necessary, the police.

Even Sasha had joined in on taking precautionary measures. Craig had begun bringing her to and picking her up from work. He had pending orders that would send him to Iraq in a few months to assist in the ongoing war there, and now he had the added worry of wondering about his wife's safety. Neither Craig nor Sasha complained, but Kelli knew it had to be a topic of discussion when they were alone. Realizing that she'd played a big role in causing the whole mess sometimes got the best of Kelli, and she'd find herself fighting tears throughout the day.

It was still almost inconceivable that a man who had been as friendly and gentle as Stuart had been could do the things that he had. A part of her still wanted to believe that she and her whole family were mistaken and that all of the things that had taken place had happened by chance. Maybe some bored, troubled kids had punctured the tires of the vehicles at the fire station. Perhaps someone else had turned on the faucet outside her parents' home.

Deep inside, though, she knew that Stuart was behind it. The look in his eyes when he gripped her arm in his hand at the bookstore coupled with the subtle threat he issued when he pulled alongside them in the park that day indicated that there was certainly another side to him.

"Earth to Kelli," Sasha called while tapping on Kelli's shoulder.

"What?"

"You know what?" Sasha said. "I think that my hubby was right. We're being way too kind to Stuart McMillian. I think we should hire a hitman and have him knocked off."

"Girl, quit playing. And don't you ever say anything like that around Jhordan. He's wanted a million times to confront Stuart. The only reason he hasn't done it is because he promised me and my father that he wouldn't."

"Kelli, all I know is if Craig, who is one of the calmest people we know, thinks that way about it, then I can only imagine what runs through Jhordan's head," Sasha remarked.

"Jhordan will be cool as long as Stuart stays away from me and my family, which he has—thank God. Mama should be picking Jazmin up from school in a little bit, and as long as he gets the call that she's okay, he'll be fine."

"How long is this going to go on, Kelli? I know this is stressful to you, but it also has to be stressful to Jhordan too. I mean, in one short year, your marriage has gone through more changes than anyone's that I know. After his first marriage, it took Jhordan years to learn to trust again, and nobody is happier that he chose you than I am. But how long can he live in a situation where he feels that Jazmin could be in danger?"

"It's going to work out, Sasha." Kelli was trying to convince herself more than her friend. "God is going to get my family through this."

"Brother Adams," Dr. Ellis said with an extended hand, "it's so good to see you. I was surprised when I got your call."

It had been weeks since Jhordan had spoken with the pastor of Mount Nebo. The last time he'd met with him, Jhordan's marriage was still slowly falling apart.

"I'm sorry that I didn't keep or call to cancel the last three appointments that I had scheduled with you," Jhordan apologized. "A lot has happened since then, and I felt it only right to give you an update."

"Good things, I hope," Dr. Ellis said as he pointed toward an empty chair, inviting Jhordan to sit. "You look well," he added. "I hope that's a good sign."

Jhordan smiled at the minister's compliment as he removed his jacket and settled in the familiar seat where he'd spent several hours in the past. "Mostly good things," he said.

"Good," Dr. Ellis said.

"I took your advice and the advice of others and opened up to Kelli about all the things that had happened in my past," Jhordan began. "All of you were right. It was the best thing to do. Because of it, we're putting our marriage back on track and trying to start with a clean slate."

"Wonderful," the pastor said. His face displayed both relief and elation.

"Since then, the marriage has hit another bump, but we're working on smoothing that out right now."

"Is that something you want to talk about?" Dr. Ellis asked. "I know this isn't an official appointment, but I'm here, and I have no other appointments today if you want to talk more about what's going on."

Without hesitation, Jhordan took advantage of the opportunity. He told the story of Kelli and Stuart and all the troubles that her brief affiliation with the lawyer had caused. Dr. Ellis listened without interruption and then leaned forward on his elbows when the story came to an end.

"Do you believe her when she says that the relationship with this fellow was purely platonic?"

"I didn't always," Jhordan admitted, "but I do now. I guess what I can't help but wonder is whether or not it would have *remained* a casual relationship had we not reconciled when we did."

"At this point, Brother Adams, that's really not important. You shouldn't spend your time wondering about what might have happened. The important thing is that God mended your relationship with your wife."

"I know," Jhordan said, "and I'm grateful for that. I never thought I'd feel this way about a woman again. Kelli's managed to put me in a place where I thought I'd never be."

"But?" Dr. Ellis said.

"But, I'm still struggling with complete trust," Jhordan said. "I'm a long way from where I was when I saw you last, but sometimes I can feel the doubt creeping up on me. Like right now," he added. "I love Kelli and can no longer imagine my life without her, but I hate the position that her actions have put me in."

"How so?"

"My father taught me a long time ago that a man isn't a man if he can't protect his family at any cost. This man that she befriended has caused harm to my family, and my hands are tied because she and her family won't let me confront him."

"It's a legal matter, Brother Adams. It's not one for you to handle."

"Nothing can be done legally," Jhordan said. "He can keep terrorizing all of us, and legally they can't do a thing without proof."

"I understand your frustrations, but even in God's Word, He commands us to be law-abiding citizens," Dr. Ellis said.

"But don't you see?" Jhordan said. "As long as this man is an active part of our lives, I'll never be able to trust in the manner which I need to. He'll always be a constant reminder of the day my wife turned to another man, for whatever reasons."

"I certainly believe that God expects us to protect our families," Dr. Ellis said, "but only if they need our protection. It seems that this man has backed away and is no longer posing a threat to you or your loved ones. I think instead of expecting the worst, you should accept that maybe God has already worked things out on your behalf. Your greatest concern should be continuing to strengthen the bond that you and your wife now have instead of pondering whether or not you have reasons to fully trust her.

"If this attorney resurfaces in a threatening manner, you can then begin looking at the best ways to handle his unwanted and unwarranted intrusions in your lives. I know that with prayer God will sustain your family."

Though Dr. Ellis made it sound much easier than it was, Jhordan left the pastor's quarters feeling somewhat encouraged. It almost seemed senseless to go back to the fire station with less than two hours remaining in his workday—especially since he was closer to home than work.

As soon as he hung up his cell phone after getting clearance to take the rest of the day off, it rang. Noting his in-laws' number on the caller ID, he answered.

"Hi, Jhordan," Mary said. "I'm just calling to let you know that Jazmin is safe with us. I just hung up with Kelli at the bookstore about a minute ago, letting her know that everything was all right. She called me before I got a chance to call you."

"Thanks so much, Mary," Jhordan said. "I may be coming to get Jazmin a little early, because I took the rest of the day off. I have a couple of things to do at home first, though."

"No hurry," Mary assured him. "She's just getting started on her homework."

"Tell her I love her," Jhordan said with a smile while turning in to his apartment complex.

"I sure will, Jhordan. She'll be happy to hear that."

As Jhordan approached his apartment, he noticed that the door was ajar. He knew that Kelli was very security conscious and would never leave the door like that, especially at a time like this. Plus, Mary had just hung up with Kelli.

"He's been to my house!" Overcome with emotions, Jhordan trembled.

"Who, Jhordan?"

"Just be sure to keep Jazmin indoors today, okay?"

"Jhordan?" Mary thought to herself that he must be talking about Stuart. She immediately went into prayer and promised herself that she wouldn't panic.

Before Mary could say anything further, Jhordan disconnected the call and stepped from his truck. In disbelief, he stared at his apartment door. Before taking another step forward, Jhordan made a complete circle—scoping out every area of his surroundings.

"Okay, God," Jhordan whispered into the air as he headed back toward his truck. "I hope You're with me on this, because ready or not—"

21

NO MORE
MR. NICE GUY

Frank McMillian, Stuart's father and the surviving co-founder of McMillian At Law, was away from the office, visiting a client in preparation for an upcoming court hearing. Dexter McMillian, Stuart's cousin and son of the deceased co-founder, had been off the entire week, trying to recover from a bout with the flu. Stuart was closed up inside of his office dictating a letter into a microcassette recorder for a client back in Atlanta.

Maya and Stephanie took advantage of the stress-free situation by doing absolutely no work while they listened carefully for sounds that indicated that Stuart would be coming out of his chambers. Files and other paperwork were already in place on the desks for them to create an illusion of multitasking if he did.

"Now, see, *this* is what I'm talking about right here," Maya said as she pointed at a picture of a bare-chested image of LL Cool J on the pages of an entertainment magazine. "Umph, umph, umph," she grunted. "I'd drink his bathwater anyday."

"I'm not saying the boy ain't put together well," Stephanie said while peering at the picture over her reading glasses. "I just can't get with these half-naked so-called singers. Whatever happened to the toned-down sexy images of the likes of Marvin Gaye and Sam Cooke? Why don't we ever see them in magazines?"

"Don't quote me on this, Steph, but I'd say we don't see much of them because they're *dead*," Maya said in sarcasm.

"What about that boy you was looking at in that magazine the other day?" Stephanie pointed out. He's been dead for years, and they had him on the front cover."

"Tupac is *not* dead, okay?" Maya said. "And let's just be real," she continued. "Not in the past or in the present has there ever been any man with a body to compete with LL's."

The front door of the business swung open, startling both women. Jhordan stood quietly in the doorway for a moment and allowed his gaze to slowly travel every square foot of the front office spacing.

"Okay, I just lied," Maya said under her breath while looking at their visitor in a mixture of fright and approval from head to toe.

"May we help you, sir?" Stephanie asked nervously, placing her hand on top of the phone as though she was preparing to call for help, if necessary.

"I need to see Attorney McMillian," Jhordan said.

"We have three Attorney McMillians," Stephanie told him. Noting Jhordan's tone and demeanor, she continued. "All of them are out of the office right now, but you can leave a message if you'd like."

"No, I would *not* like to leave a message," Jhordan said harshly.

Quickly, Stephanie picked up the telephone and began dialing 911. Jhordan rushed to the desk where they both stood and forced the telephone from her hand before hanging it back up.

"Oh, God help us," Stephanie gasped as she stepped away.

"I'm sorry," Jhordan apologized, somewhat calming her. "I'm very sorry. I don't mean to frighten you, and I'm not here to do any harm—not to you anyway," he added. "However, it is *very* important that I see him, and if I have to sit here and wait for Stuart McMillian to return, I will."

"Oh, *him?*" Maya said with a turned-up lip. "He's right in there," she pointed toward Stuart's closed door. "Go right on in, my brotha."

Without a moment's hesitation, Jhordan followed the direction of her finger and walked toward the door. The force he used to push it open nearly jolted it from its frame.

"What the . . ." Stuart said in surprise. "Who are you?"

"My name is Jhordan Adams," Jhordan introduced himself while still standing in the open entranceway to Stuart's office. "I believe you know my wife!"

"Call the police!" Stuart yelled just before Jhordan slammed the door behind him, closing the two of them inside the room.

Stephanie and Maya exchanged glances while they gave the frantic request some thought.

"Yeah, right," they both said before rushing to the door and pressing their ears against it for a clearer reception.

On the other side, Jhordan had snatched the telephone

from Stuart's reach and jerked the plug from its socket. With no place to run or hide, the attorney's back was against the wall as he watched the man, whom he clearly was no match for, approach him.

"What do you want?"

"I know what happened with you and my wife," Jhordan said. "She told me the whole story."

"How you gonna come in here threatening me?" Stuart demanded through the fear he tried to hide. "You're the one who cheated on her."

"I *never* cheated on her!" Jhordan said through clinched teeth. "I don't have to prove anything to you. That's not what I'm here for."

"I want you out of my office," Stuart said.

"And I want you out of my life!" Jhordan said. "When you broke into my apartment, you stepped over the line. Actually, when you first hit on my wife, that was your first mistake.

"You can't prove that I did anything," Stuart said.

"You're right," Jhordan said. "I can't prove it. If I could, you'd be a lawyer *needing* a lawyer. I can't prove it, but I know it's true, and so do you. You've stalked my wife, confronted her on her job, damaged my in-laws' property, slashed the tires of my truck, and now you've gone too far."

"You think you have it all figured out, don't you?" Stuart said. "You're here because you're jealous! You're mad because your wife looked at me and saw something she didn't see in you. Kelli deserves better than you. She's a cum laude college graduate who owns a successful business. Look at you," he continued with a sneer. "You're nothing but an average blue-collar workin' brotha. You've got *nothing*. You're a fireman—a water hose with muscles—all brawn and no brain."

Stuart's grin quickly faded as Jhordan struck him across the jaw, sending him tumbling over a large potted plant and onto the floor. He slowly staggered back to his feet with the help of a corner table and wiped away the blood that dripped from his mouth.

"My secretaries have called the police," he said through pants of breath, "and in just a few seconds, you'll be leaving here in handcuffs."

"If one of us is going to jail, my friend," Jhordan said, "it's gonna be you."

"On what grounds?" Stuart said with a laugh. "I'm a lawyer. I know the system. So what if I did all the things you're accusing me of? You have to be able to prove it before a jury in a court of law, and you can't. This blood," he said as he held out his opened hand, "is proof that you hit me. That's assault. You need more than a high school diploma to battle with me, jungle boy. You're out of your league with me and Kelli.

"And while you're pointing blame," Stuart continued, wiping more blood, "keep in mind that nobody in your family, your little girl included, would have had to go through any of this if it hadn't been for you. *You're* the reason all of this happened. None of it would have taken place *if you had taken care of business at home.*"

You're the reason. It was the phrase his mother had used—blaming him for her taking her own life. It was the phrase Sadonia had used—blaming him for the reason that their marriage failed. The third time was one too many.

"Let me tell you something," Jhordan said angrily, grabbing Stuart by the neck and pressing his back against the wall. "I'm about *this* close," he said, using his thumb and index finger from his opposite hand for visual aid, "to breaking my foot off up in your cocky behind."

Stuart's face reddened because of the lack of oxygen as he struggled madly to free himself. Strength for strength, he was no match for his opponent. Feeling his rage suddenly draining from him and his spiritual conscience taking over, Jhordan loosed his grip and watched his enemy slide to the floor, gasping for breath.

"Stay away from my family," Jhordan whispered harshly. "Stay away," he repeated the warning slowly this time, "from my family."

Maya and Stephanie scrambled away from the door and made poor attempts to appear nonchalant as Jhordan stepped from Stuart's office. Seeing them standing nearby, Jhordan stopped and turned to face them.

"I apologize for my entrance, ladies," he started.

"Don't mention it. Forget about it. No problem. You a'iight. We're cool." They both spoke concurrently. Jhordan wasn't sure which of them said what, but he nodded appreciatively and made a much calmer exit.

"Mama, why didn't you call me earlier?" Kelli demanded into her cell phone as she pulled from the parking lot and headed toward McMillian At Law.

"'Cause I knew you weren't gonna listen to me when I told you to stay out of it," Mary said. "Your daddy and Tony are already taking care of it. They headed out toward your house awhile ago."

"Jhordan's probably not at the house, Mama. If anything, he's over there beating the fool out of Stuart right now. Jhordan was struggling to contain himself as it was. I'm sure there's no more Mr. Nice Guy left in him after Stuart's latest stunt."

"Good for him."

"Mama, Jhordan could get locked up for doing something like that!" Kelli said tearfully. "I can't let him go to jail because of something I caused. But I know he'll do it—especially when Jazmin is involved."

"Let's just pray it don't come to that," Mary said.

"I gotta go," Kelli said. "I'm here now."

"Call me and let me know what you find out," Mary told her.

Kelli stepped cautiously from her car and looked at the office building in front of her. She saw two cars in the parking lot—one of them being the Mercedes that Stuart drove. She took a deep breath and said a silent prayer before walking inside the office and seeing the two women gathered around a desk with their faces bent closely to it.

The ringing of the bell that dangled from the top of the door brought them to a standing position. Kelli saw Maya tuck something behind her back while Stephanie rounded the desk and faced their newest visitor.

"May we help you?" she asked.

"Yes," Kelli said as the door opened again behind her. She turned to see her father and Tony walking in. "This is some of my family." She paused to introduce them. "We're not sure that he's actually been here, but I'm looking for my husband."

"Tall, dark, and fine with an accent?" Maya spoke up.

"He's been here?" Wesley asked.

"Yes," Stephanie said, "but he's gone now."

"Was there any . . . trouble?" Tony asked.

"Not as far as we're concerned," Maya said with a short laugh.

"Shhh!" Stephanie said, glancing behind her. "Mr. McMillian is in the bathroom down the hall, and he probably wouldn't be too happy to see you all here. You'd better leave," she advised.

"I understand," Wesley said. "Were the police involved?"

"No." Stephanie shook her head. "He asked us to call them, but we didn't. He's really upset with us about that right now. He had us take Polaroid photos of his face and of his office. He said he's going to the police as soon as he leaves work. Your husband left a pretty bad bruise on him."

"Oh, goodness," Kelli whispered as she covered her face with her hands.

"Take this," Maya said. Revealing the hand that she had hidden behind her back, she handed them a small tape recorder. "He was dictating a letter when your husband got here, and he never turned it off when they were arguing. We found it on the floor when we were taking pictures in there. The whole conversation was recorded. I think this will be all the police need to hear."

"Thank You, Jesus," Wesley whispered as he took the recorder from her hand.

"He admitted everything?" Kelli asked hopefully.

"Just take it and go!" Stephanie whispered upon hearing noises from the rear of the building.

"Thank you," Tony said.

"Yes," Kelli said as she quickly hugged both women. "Thank you, so much."

Immediately upon leaving the law firm, the three of them stopped by the police station and filed a formal complaint—using the tape as evidence. They were told by the police chief that a warrant for Stuart's arrest would be issued and that he would be arrested as soon as they located him. The relief that Kelli felt was short-lived. They were also warned that Stuart would most likely be able to get the monies together to post bail and be able to continue working until the hearing was scheduled.

"This is all my fault," Kelli said in a burst of tears once they were outside the police station.

"Like I tell my students," Tony said as he embraced her, "making mistakes is actually a good thing when you come out with a lesson learned."

"Amen," Wesley agreed.

22

AIN'T NO RIVER

*D*ear Kelli,
    Under the circumstances, I didn't think that this trip would be a wise one for us to take together. I'd rather there be no friction between us whenever we visit Papa for the first time together. I know that you are not pleased with me right now, and most likely, neither are the members of your family. I broke the agreement that I'd made with your father and with you not to take matters into my own hands concerning this whole situation. I make no excuses, and I have no misgivings. If I could do it all over again, I'd do it the same way, even though I realize that at this point in time I'm a wanted man for my actions. No, it solved nothing, but I feel vindicated to a degree. I couldn't remain silent a moment longer. I couldn't sit quietly and let him continue to intimidate our family.

    I took Jazmin, and we left a day early to head to Trinidad. I needed to get away from everything, and for safety purposes, I wanted to take her with me. I'd appreciate it if you would spend the next few days with your parents so that you won't be home alone. I will return after Jeanette's wedding and Carnival has ended.

I do love you, and I hope you can forgive me. I hope we can forgive each other.

In love, I remain,
Jhordan

Kelli was finally alone. All of her family had spent the last several hours with her. At midnight her parents, who were the last to leave, hugged her and reminded her to lock the doors and set her alarm. True to their word, the police had placed Stuart under arrest when he walked into the station to try and press charges against Jhordan. He would remain in jail at least throughout the weekend, they said, until his hearing on Monday. Still, she knew that Jhordan would be unhappy to know that she'd gone against his wishes and was spending the night alone.

She placed the handwritten letter that Jhordan had left for her on the dresser beside the bed and curled into a fetal position under her covers, staring at the clock on the nightstand. Jazmin's fear had come to pass. The picture that she drew of her dream of watching her parents swim in the lake while she and her grandfather's dog looked on would not be realized after all.

Apparently, upon leaving McMillian At Law, Jhordan had headed straight to his mother-in-law's house and picked up his daughter. Mary said that he had been visibly upset, but since she had been aware of what had just transpired, she hadn't been surprised by his demeanor. He had made no mention to her, however, that he would be stopping by his home just long enough to pack a few items and write the note for Kelli before beginning the journey by air that would take him more than twelve hours.

She had been anxiously planning and looking forward to meeting her in-laws and establishing a more personal relationship with them. In the year that she and Jhordan had been married, she'd spoken to Jeanette on a few occasions and his father during two separate phone calls that Jhordan had made to him. Her only connection to his other sisters was the pictures in the photo album that Jhordan kept on their bookshelf. Kelli was familiar with the story of how Napoleon Adams had never cared much for the first bride that his son had chosen. She knew that Sadonia never made an effort to bond with Jhordan's relatives. The last thing Kelli wanted was for her father-in-law or Jhordan's siblings to think the same way about her.

The numbers on the digital clock changed as she looked on. It was 2:00 in the morning. Another four hours and Jhordan and Jazmin would be unloading at Crown Point Airport without her. Worst of all, he'd left his cell phone on the bed on top of the note. Not knowing the country code or Napoleon's phone number, Kelli had no way of contacting him, and, apparently, he wanted it that way.

The sounds of her telephone ringing startled her. Kelli sat straight up in the bed and stared into the darkness of her bedroom. At the second ring, she looked at the caller ID and momentarily froze at the sight of Sadonia's name and number.

"Go away," she said aloud as she turned her back to the telephone and pressed the side of her head back into the pillow.

The fifth ring brought her back to a seated position. The answering machine should have picked up on the fourth ring. That was the default setting that she and Jhordan had never changed. On the tenth ring, and almost involuntarily, she reached for the phone and placed it to her ear.

"Hello."

A brief silence followed. "Kelli?" Sadonia finally spoke.

"Yes?"

"I'm sorry to be calling so late," she said, "but I really need to speak with Jhordan."

"He's not available," Kelli said.

"Please," Sadonia said. Her voice was kind, and her tone was earnest. "I know that it's an awful hour, and I also understand why you wouldn't want me speaking with him. I upset him and you too, I'm sure, during my last visit. I'm sorry," Sadonia said. Kelli heard soft sniffles through the telephone. Sadonia was crying.

"My intentions were wrong for coming there," she continued. "He was right; it wasn't about Jazmin. I mean, it was nice to see her—I'm always happy to see my baby— but I didn't really come for that purpose. I came to see *him*."

Kelli wasn't sure how to respond. A part of her wanted to be angry and lash out at Sadonia for her deceptive tactics. She wanted to tell her what a poor excuse for a mother she was to use her daughter as a pawn to get close to a man she willingly left. But instead she remained quiet and allowed Sadonia to continue speaking.

"I was wrong," Sadonia said. "But I just thought I'd give it one last try. I wore an outfit that I was sure would catch his eyes. I even got my hair cut in the style that he used to love—just because I was going to be seeing him. None of it mattered," she said tearfully. "He didn't notice any of it. All I saw in his eyes was contempt. None of it mattered," she repeated.

"You came to get him back?" Kelli asked.

"Yes," Sadonia admitted following a short pause. "And I'm sorry for that. He didn't deserve my intrusion," she said. "*You* didn't deserve my intrusion."

"Do you now love him again?" It was a question that Kelli had always wanted to know the answer to, but had never bothered to ask Jhordan. Maybe it was because she didn't have the courage, or maybe it was because she was unsure if she even wanted to know the answer.

"I never stopped loving him," Sadonia said with little hesitation. "I didn't walk away because I didn't love him. I walked away because love wasn't enough for me. I wanted love, but I wanted money even more. I loved Jhordan way more than I ever loved Pete, but I thought that the money would make up for wherever my feelings for Pete fell short.

"It was the biggest mistake of my life," she said. "But I think I've finally accepted that you are the woman he loves and that I'll never have a chance to right the wrong that I did. What I did was too damaging to rectify. Jhordan will always hate me."

"He doesn't hate you, Sadonia," Kelli said. She was surprised by the compassion that she felt for the woman on the other end of the line, especially because of Sadonia's admission of what her intentions were initially. Sadonia's honesty was oddly refreshing, and for the first time, Kelli didn't feel threatened by the woman who'd once owned her husband's heart.

"I think he hated you for a time," she continued, "but not anymore. Jhordan has come a long way, and getting over what happened with you was very hard for him. I don't think the two of you will ever be friends, but he doesn't hate you."

"Well, he should," Sadonia replied, her tears still audible. "Do you know our story? Do you know what I put him through?"

"Yes."

"Wouldn't you hate me?"

Kelli stopped and thought for a moment. The answer immediately on her lips wouldn't make the situation any better. Instead she said, "A wise man once told me that making mistakes is actually a good thing when you come out having learned a lesson. It was a terrible thing that happened, but it wasn't beyond forgiveness—and God's forgiveness is more important than that of anyone else."

"Please let me speak to him," Sadonia said.

"I wasn't trying to prevent you from talking to him before," Kelli said. "He's not here."

"He's not there?" she questioned. "I thought he'd be in from work by now."

Kelli inhaled deeply. Jhordan's whereabouts really weren't any business of Sadonia's, but she felt a strange need to talk right now, and the unlikely ears belonged to Sadonia.

"He's not at work," she said. "He's on his way to Trinidad for Carnival."

Sadonia was quiet for several moments. Kelli knew that she was reminiscing again, most likely about the one year that she'd been privileged to attend the festivities with her then husband.

"I forgot about Carnival," Sadonia finally said. "They go to that every year. Jazmin mentioned it when she was here. I thought she said that *all* of you were going to attend. You didn't go?"

It was Kelli's turn for silence. She wanted to tell Sadonia that she'd decided not to go or tell her that something came up that prevented her from being able to make the trip, but it would have all been a lie. Still, she couldn't

216

bring herself to tell her husband's ex-wife of the events that had caused her to be left behind. Her mind raced, but a quick answer escaped her.

"Listen to me, Kelli," Sadonia said after Kelli's extended quietness. "I don't know what's going on, and it's not my business. But one thing I know for sure is that Jhordan and Jazmin love you. You're all she talks about when she's here with me," she said with a tremble in her voice, "and Jhordan has repeatedly told me how he feels about you.

"When I first found out about your engagement, I called to try and stop it. He told me in no uncertain terms that he'd found the woman who could give him what he thought he could never have. He loves you, Kelli, and I know you love him."

"We're not breaking up, Sadonia," Kelli said. "Everything is going to be okay. We're just working through some things. We're not breaking up at all. Everything will be fine as soon as he gets back home."

When the call ended, Kelli's thoughts didn't. Sadonia's words echoed in her ear and Kelli knew what she had to do. Ain't no river wide enough to keep us apart, she thought.

23

THAT FAITH,
THAT TRUST, THAT LOVE

Having gotten very little sleep and with little time to spare before she needed to be at the airport, Kelli packed the last items into her bag. The large carry-on bag would be her only piece of luggage. She didn't want to overpack, realizing that there was a very good chance that Jhordan could send her right back home.

Three changes of casual clothing, a dress to wear to Jeanette's wedding, two pairs of shoes, two nightgowns, a swimsuit, her camera, and one small gift were fit snugly into the shoulder bag.

Kelli had never been a fan of flying. Since the 9/11 attacks a few years ago, she couldn't be convinced that the skies would ever be friendly again. As a matter of fact, she always feared the idea of soaring above the land with nothing between the plane and the ground except air. The two times that she'd flown previously, the trips had been short, and there was always someone traveling with her.

"I can't lie, Daddy," Kelli had told him early that morning upon informing both her parents of her sudden decision to follow Jhordan. "I'm scared to death of this trip. Can't you come with me? At least one of you?"

"We can't, baby," Wesley had said. "Your mama has to keep Christopher and Tonya while your sister and Tony are working, and you know I have to help with putting the new carpet down in the church tomorrow. I already promised that I'd help. I can't pull out now. If you don't feel comfortable, then maybe you shouldn't go. Jhordan will be back in a few days."

"No, I need to go," Kelli had said. "I'll be fine. I guess there's a first for everything."

"Let her 'lone, Wesley," her mother had said to Kelli's surprise. "She'll make it there just fine."

If either of her parents were going to be against her decision to fly alone, Kelli fully expected it to be her mother. When she drove alone to Miami, Florida, two years ago to attend a funeral of a former classmate who had died in a tragic accident, Mary made her disapproval known. She did a "let the dead bury the dead" speech that lasted for two days, which Kelli didn't see as relevant to her situation. It seemed unbelievable that she was insisting that she make a nearly thirteen-hour flight to another country.

"She messed up," Mary had continued. "I knew somewhere 'long down the line that strong head of yours was gonna be your downfall," she had said to Kelli.

"Mama—"

"Hush, now," her mother had scolded. "I ain't blaming you for everything. I played my part in making Jhordan feel a little inadequate at times myself. Both of us did him wrong, but when you got caught up with that lawyer, you straight up showed your behind. You never should have paid him no attention. Now look at where he is and *what* he is. All that glitters definitely ain't gold."

"Mary," Wesley had warned.

"Am I lying?" Mary had asked. "No. Look at what a difference a day makes. Already we done found out from our attorney that Stuart McMillian got a wife that he's still married to back in Atlanta who had to get a restraining order placed against him when she broke up with him. The man is crazy, and if it wasn't for the Lord, this whole thing could have been a lot worse."

"I know, Mama," Kelli had said.

"You messed up," her mother had reiterated.

"She knows that, Mary," Wesley had said while moving to the other side of the room in hopes of gaining some peace as he attempted to read the newspaper.

"Now, here you are just a few hours away from your first anniversary, and what you doin'?" she had asked. "Sitting here looking like a sick chicken instead of being in Trinidad meeting your family like you was supposed to be doing today."

Kelli had felt as though she'd somehow stepped into a time machine and gone back about fifteen years. The last time her mother had delivered her a scolding like this, she'd been just shy of her fifteenth birthday. Kelli had had no license or learner's permit, but on the dare of some neighborhood school friends, she'd gotten behind the wheel of her best friend's mother's car and driven around the block.

Cheryl had spotted her and run home to tell their parents. As a fourteen-year-old ninth-grade honor student, Kelli had gotten the lecture of her life and a whipping to go along with it. Sometimes the lashes of the lecture were more painful.

"I know Jhordan had his issues too," Mary had said,

"but you *knew* he had issues when you married him, and you married him anyway. When you did that and took those vows, you were telling God that you could handle whatever it was that your husband was dealing with. You knew about Jhordan's issues. He didn't know about yours. He didn't know that you would run to another man and get the whole family in a mess at the first sign of trouble.

"Kelli, if you want that faith, that trust, that love—all the wonderful stuff that God has to offer in a marriage—you got to stand strong, and when anything at all comes up that troubles you, you're gonna have to go to Jhordan and talk to *him*. Not Sasha, not Stuart, not nobody else. You got to talk to *him*.

"Y'all young girls today don't know nothing 'bout how to treat a good man," Mary had continued. "That's why half of today's marriages end in divorce. Y'all want to always point the finger at the man, but from where I'm standing the men are looking pretty good. Look at Sister Cook," Mary had ranted on. "Had a good husband who worked hard so she could stay home and be a housewife. But noooo—she wanted more. Now what she got? Nothing—that's what she got. I bet you every single morning when she got to go to the old folks' home and change them grown folks' stanking diapers, she wish to God she'd been good to that man.

"God let you catch a *good* fish that another woman was dumb enough to throw back in the water. She knows she was dumb too; that's why she told you what she told you last night. Every time she looks in the mirror, I bet she sees the word 'dummy' written right 'cross her forehead in bold red letters. And look at you. You went and stood right on the edge of being dummy number two. Is that what you want to be, Kelli—dummy number two?"

"No, Mama." Kelli had sighed.

"Then what you waiting for?" her mother had asked. "Go home, pack your bags, and get to Trinidad. Don't pay your daddy no attention. You ain't gonna be by yourself. God will be with you. He'll take you there, and He'll bring you back.

"All you need to focus on is finding your husband. And when you find him, you let him know that he's not in any legal trouble for protecting his family. Tell him we got a good lawyer, and he ain't got nothing to worry about. And while you're talking, tell him that you messed up, you're sorry, and it won't happen again. Go on," she had urged with a wave of her hand.

The lecture had ended. Kelli had stood and hugged her mother tightly, not sure whether she'd been hugging her in appreciation for sharing the mountain of words that were on her mind or in appreciation for finally dismissing her from the brutal tongue-lashing. Either way, she loved her and knew that her mother loved her right back.

"Thanks, Mama," she had said.

"Uh-huh." Mary had returned her hug. "Now get going. And if you don't come back with my son-in-law and my granddaughter, don't bother coming back at all."

"Be careful, baby," Wesley had said when it was his turn to embrace his daughter. "Call us when you get settled."

On her way home from her visit with her parents, Kelli had stopped by her bookstore and picked up the present she'd purchased and gift wrapped two days ago in preparation for their anniversary.

Kelli had noticed her cell phone blinking at the bottom of her purse, indicating that she had a message waiting. She hadn't recalled hearing her phone ring, but then again it probably had happened while her mother was giving Kelli a piece of her mind.

As Kelli had listened to the message, she heard her sister-in-law Jeanette's voice. She told Kelli that she didn't know what had transpired between her and Jhordan, but that she'd been waiting to meet Kelli and wanted her at the wedding. Jeanette had given Kelli all the phone numbers and addresses and other pertinent information that she would need to make the trip. She also made it clear that Jhordan knew nothing about the call.

The tongue-lashing from her mother and Jeanette's call had been all the confirmation that Kelli had needed to make the trip.

In spite of the somewhat dismal situation surrounding the need for her trip, as she maneuvered through the airport, everything Kelli saw seemed to remind her of her husband and made her want to be with him even more.

The man at the ticket counter was tall and dark and spoke with a defined accent. When asked about his heritage, he proudly told her that he was from Barbados. Passing the fire exits, she thought of what Jhordan did on a daily basis, and the extended lines at the security checkpoints and armed officers throughout the airport reminded her of September 11 and the lives that her husband had helped to save.

Butterflies gathered in the pit of Kelli's stomach as she finally boarded the plane and settled back in her assigned seat and buckled herself in. Looking out at the view of the airport on her right, she wondered why she had asked for a window seat.

"Best seat in the house," the man who sat next to her remarked with a smile.

Kelli smiled back but couldn't agree with him less.

However, having sat in the middle seat both times when she'd flown before, she would agree that her seat was better than his. If the view of the outside became too much, she could always close the window shade. For him, there was no relief from being sandwiched in the middle.

Early in the flight, Kelli's body reminded her of its lack of sleep. Putting her earphones on, she turned on her portable CD player, leaned back, and prepared herself for the long ride ahead.

24

RHYTHMS

For years the rustling of the water at the popular fishermen's pier had been a source of peace and serenity for Jhordan. He'd stood there for hours after the death of his mother and had returned after his divorce from Sadonia. Both times, the view of the reflection of the sun or moon against the murky waters had somehow brought a sense of calm to the battle in his heart.

"Is it working?"

Jhordan quietly shook his head. He sighed heavily before turning to face the cigar-smoking man who was all too familiar with the heartbreaks that Jhordan had endured over the years.

"You need to go back and get her." The thick-accented, prematurely gray-haired man reiterated the advice he'd been trying to hand Jhordan for the past several hours.

"I can't do that, Papa," Jhordan told his father. "I can't put myself out there like that."

Napoleon Adams was a relatively young man, not yet sixty years old. Jhordan had always been close to his father, but since moving to the States, he only saw him once or twice a year.

"You shouldn't have ever left her there to begin with. You jumped the gun," his father scolded through a puff of thick smoke. "I understand your reasoning, but a man doesn't leave a letter to say what's on his heart. That's what cowards do. I didn't raise no coward, no?"

"No," Jhordan said. "You're right." He looked out and saw the car carrying Jazmin and his three sisters, Naomi, Imani, and Jeanette pulling into the yard. "I'll call her as soon as we return."

"Daddy, Daddy!" Jazmin called as she jumped out of the car and ran to him. "We had fun at Aunt Naomi's house."

"Very good, sweetheart," Jhordan said, trying to smile through his aching heart. He missed his wife, and he tried hard to avoid the disappointing eyes of his siblings, who had all had high hopes of meeting her.

"Are you ready to tear down de roof?" Jeanette asked him.

"It's been awhile," Jhordan said, smiling, "but I think I can handle it."

Trinidad didn't celebrate February American holidays such as Valentine's Day, but every year around the same time there would be something festive going on. Jhordan and his father had spent the early morning hours working together to complete a rocking chair for Old Man Carlos. Napoleon had always been good with building things.

By the early afternoon, they were dressed in bright outfits and ready to head to Port of Spain for Panorama, the national steel band competition. It was a most an-

ticipated time of year as the people of Trinidad and Tobago took to the streets for days of music, dancing, pa-
rades, competitions and good food.

"Hold your chin up now, boy," Napoleon said to him
as they arrived at their destination and climbed out of
his van. The streets were already crowded, and the fun
had already begun. "You play," he added while pointing to Jhordan's instrument. "You play happy music and
think happy thoughts. Then when we're all finished, you
call her and make amends."

Jhordan forced a smile and nodded in silent agreement. His father made it sound so much simpler than it
was, but deep inside he knew the lively, older version of
himself was right. His leaving Kelli behind was wrong,
and he had to be a man about it and admit it.

No one outside of his native country knew how
skilled Jhordan was at playing steel pan music. Next to
running and basketball, it had been his favorite childhood
activity. His instrument was called the double second
pans. The double drum carried the alto tune of whatever
band it was played in. The expensive piece of equipment
would cost almost four thousand American dollars to
buy, but his father worked in the industry years ago and
had made it for Jhordan when he was a teenager. When
he moved to the States, he'd left it at his father's house for
safekeeping but returned every year to fine-tune his skills.

The aching for Kelli's presence was temporarily
pushed aside as Jhordan and Jazmin got into the spirit
of the festivities. Some old friends recognized them as they
made their way through the crowd.

"Jhordan!" one of the men in his old band called. "We
didn't think you'd make it this year, old married man,"
he joked. "Come join us!"

Jhordan smiled as he headed toward the stage of

musicians. All of the other band members had been together and practicing since the end of Christmas. Jhordan would catch on. He always did.

Napoleon led Jazmin in a jovial dance while his son joined the others in a rhythm of highly energetic tunes. His daughters cheered them on, laughing at their father's steps. The competition had begun.

Several miles away, Kelli anxiously fidgeted in the taxicab as she awaited her introduction to her new family and her reunion with her husband.

Kelli found herself sandwiched between two other women in the backseat of the taxi cab, holding her luggage in her lap. The drive seemed to take forever. By the time they arrived, the skies were beginning to darken, but the festivities were still going strong. She found a nearby portable washroom and freshened up and then called the number that Jeanette had left for her.

Noticing other people sitting on top of vehicles, she found a vacant one and sat on it to watch the festive mingling of colors. She unconsciously wagged her feet to the beat of the music as she sat.

Kelli had never seen so many people or so many bands all at one time and in one place before. Fishing her camera from her bag, she began snapping photos of the goings-on around her. The reality that she was in her husband's homeland gave her a feeling of warmth as she zoomed in on another photo opportunity.

"Sitting on the hood of my truck will cost you $5."

The voice startled Kelli. She immediately closed her camera lens and slid off of the front of the vehicle. She brushed her dress to make sure that it was down in the back and looked up into the face of the tall stranger. Dark shades covered his eyes, but his smile was friendly.

"I'm sorry," she said.

"I was kidding," he said with a laugh. "Climb on back up there. A beautiful thing like you makes this old truck look mighty good. I won't be leaving for a long while yet," he said. "I just came to get my medicine."

Kelli watched as he opened the cab of his vehicle and reached into the glove compartment. Popping the capsules into his mouth, he quickly washed them down with bottled water and then looked back at her and smiled.

"Go on," he encouraged her. "Sit back down and rest your feet."

"It's okay," Kelli said as she readjusted the shoulder strap of her bag on her shoulder. "I can stand."

"You have luggage. You're not from here," he observed.

"No, sir."

"The States?"

"Yes, sir."

"Well, welcome to Trinidad," he said with an outstretched hand. "You look a bit lost. Are you here alone?"

"For now, yes," she said. "I was looking for . . . some old friends."

"Well, I am a new friend," he said, "and until you find your old ones, why don't you join me in a dance, yes?"

"No, thank you," she said shyly. "I don't even know you."

"Then we can remedy that, can't we?" he said, laughing. "First of all, I'm not a dirty old man. I'm a hardworking decent human being, and I have a face you can trust. Don't you agree?"

"I guess." Kelli returned his friendly smile.

"Here, you can see it better now," he said as he removed his dark shades. "My name is Napoleon. What's yours?"

Kelli stared at him. Suddenly the eyes combined with the dimple-chinned smile made him share a familiar look.

"Did you forget your name?" he teased.

"Napoleon?" she asked slowly. "Napoleon Adams?"

It was Napoleon's turn to be taken aback. He searched the face of the strange girl who knew his family name.

"Yes," he said slowly. "How did you know that? Should I know you?"

Just then, Kelli's cell phone rang.

"Hello, Jeanette?"

Napoleon looked puzzled hearing his daughter's name.

"Yes, Kelli, where are you?"

"I'm standing here next to the entrance talking to your dad. I guess we're on our way to meet everyone!"

Hanging up the phone, she turned to Napoleon. "My name is Kelli." She blinked back tears. "I'm your . . ."

"Daughter-in-law?" he finished her sentence.

"Yes."

"Well, I'll be." He smiled broadly before bringing her in for a long hug. "My, my, my," he said, stepping back and looking at her with approval. "My Jhordan said you were almost too beautiful to look at, and he didn't lie."

"Thank you." Kelli blushed and fought back overwhelming emotions. "Oh, my goodness," she said. "You're my father-in-law. I'm so glad to meet you."

"Stop with the tears now, girl." Napoleon laughed. He removed her bag from her shoulder and placed it in his van before locking and closing the door. "Come with me."

Hand in hand the two edged their way through the celebrators. Kelli laughed as Napoleon occasionally stopped to get in a few dance steps with several bopping ladies that they encountered during their journey.

As they finally made it to the area where the stage sat he stopped and proceeded to break into a full-fledged tango-type dance with a beautiful full-figured woman who danced like she had it going on. Her hips swayed so strongly that, had her skirt been any shorter, she probably would have taken all the attention away from the actual performers.

As entertaining as it was, Kelli just wanted to find Jazmin and Jhordan. The crowd was too thick to find a noticeable face. Napoleon twirled his partner and smiled when he caught Kelli's eyes. Silently, he pointed toward the stage that was at least fifty feet ahead of them.

Kelli studied the stage carefully. The dreadlocked lead singer pranced across the platform as he sang. In the back corner of the stage were his background singers, which consisted of two men and three women who sang with him and moved in synchronized motions. Beside them were the musicians, who played feverishly and tirelessly to the apparent crowd favorite tune of "Tear Down de Roof."

"On the far right!" Napoleon yelled in her ear while continuing his dance.

Kelli finally focused in on the sun-kissed man in white closest to the end of the stage. She gasped. Her eyes dropped to the little girl who, with skirt tail in hand, danced around his legs. It was a wonderful sight to behold. She laughed and clapped through threatening tears.

Just as she focused her lens in close and snapped a second photo, Napoleon grabbed her arm and spun her around. She had never done the joyous-looking dances that the Trinidadians and Tobagonians were doing, but it didn't look much different than the shout that Mother Brown did every other Sunday at church. Normally, Kelli would shy away and decline the dance, but she'd found Jhordan and her daughter, and she was too happy not to join her father-in-law in the celebration.

For a man of his maturity, Napoleon had a lot of energy. He was light on his feet and laughed as she stumbled over hers in an attempt to keep up with him. Carnival was the longest but most festive party Kelli had ever taken part in.

As nightfall finally crept in, the band began disassembling. It was then that Kelli realized that the bands hadn't just been entertaining them, but it was also a competition. Winners were announced, but Jhordan's band wasn't one of them. No one seemed to care. Having fun seemed to have been the ultimate goal, and they'd reached it hours ago.

There was still plenty of music going on elsewhere, but Jhordan and his friends had apparently tired out. Neither he nor his daughter had seen Kelli among the throng of onlookers, and Napoleon saw an opportunity he couldn't pass up. Motioning with his hand for Kelli to keep her distance, they started toward the stage where Jhordan was using a white handkerchief to wipe the sweat from his and Jazmin's face.

As silently instructed, Kelli stood at the foot of the stage while Jhordan's father walked up the steps to join them.

"I was dancing, Papa," Jazmin told him. "Did you see me? I was dancing!"

"Yes, you were." He hugged her. "And you danced better than everybody here. All by yourself, you deserved that award," he boasted.

"I know." She nodded happily in agreement.

"I told you a little music was all you needed to lift your spirits," Napoleon told his son.

"Yes," Jhordan said. "It was good medicine for the moment. Maybe all the activity will help me to finally sleep tonight."

"I have the feeling you will sleep just fine, my boy," he patted Jhordan's back.

"But first I have to call Kelli," Jhordan reminded him.

"Can I talk to Mommy, Daddy?" Jazmin pleaded. "Please. I want to tell her about my dance and how much we miss her and that we wish we had brought her with us."

"I think I should be the one to tell her that, sweetie," Jhordan said as he knelt down to tie her shoelaces.

Kelli covered her lips with her hands to stifle the outburst of emotion that she felt building up inside of her.

"I think you should do one better," Napoleon said. "I think you should talk to her face-to-face. I think you should see her."

"I have three more days here, Papa," Jhordan said. "I can't leave before Jeanette's wedding. She'd never forgive me. And going to get Kelli and coming back in time for the wedding would be too rushed, and it would cost too much money. A phone call will have to do."

"What if you didn't have to fly to the States?" his father said.

"What do you mean?" Jhordan asked.

"I mean, what if she was here?" he said. "Right here. Right now."

Jhordan looked at his father in a mixture of confusion and suspicion. He followed the direction of his outstretched hand and saw Kelli appear from the bottom of the stage. Slowly, from his bent-knee position, he stood and faced her from his place on top of the stage.

"Mommy!"

Jazmin dashed around her grandfather and down the steps. Kelli caught her in her arms and released her tears on the little girl's shoulder.

"I'm sorry," she whispered in Jazmin's ear. "Mommy is sorry for everything."

"I'm sorry too." Jazmin patted her back and tried to comfort her, not even aware of why she or Kelli were apologizing.

The other musicians who had been dismantling their own equipment stopped and took note of the display that was going on beside them. Jhordan hadn't moved from the place where he stood. Napoleon extended a hand to help Kelli as she placed Jazmin on the ground and made her way up the stairs to meet his son.

"I'm sorry, but I had to come," she said softly through lingering tears. "I know you didn't want me to be here. I know you didn't want to see me, but I had to see you. I had to be with you."

"No, sweetheart," Jhordan said as he wiped her tears with his hands. "I'm glad you're here. I'm the one who owes *you* an apology. I'm sorry I left you alone. I'll never leave you alone again."

"Happy anniversary," Kelli whispered.

"Happy anniversary," he whispered back.

The noise of the music and dancing in the distance and the racket of the instruments as the fellow musicians went back to their task was lost in the lingering kiss that was shared by the reunited couple. Napoleon grabbed the abandoned steel drum and took Jazmin's hand.

"How about we load up the truck?" he whispered.

"We can't just *leave* them here," Jazmin whispered back.

"Your daddy knows where the truck is. They can join us later. Let's find your aunties."

Looking through the crowd, Napoleon motioned for Jeanette and pointed at Jhordan and Kelli as if to say, "There they are."

"Okay," Jazmin conceded as she took one last glance at them over her shoulder. "'Cause they might be awhile."

25

CROSSING
JHORDAN'S RIVER

The family had finally retired inside of Napoleon's house. After returning from the happenings at Carnival, they'd spent hours swimming in Old Man Carlos' lake. There were far more people in the lake than were in Jazmin's picture, but the little girl didn't seem to mind, as she spent most of her time on dry ground, trying with little success to get Mutton to chase after her.

The bathroom, still the only one in the house, stayed occupied as each of them changed into dry clothes before assembling in the living room to further enjoy one another's company.

Kelli wasn't sure what Jhordan's father was cooking in the kitchen, but whatever it was, it filled the house with a delicious aroma that her still-empty stomach yearned for. The long day had finally taken its toll on Jazmin. She'd fallen asleep on the sofa, and Jhordan had excused himself to prepare her for bed, which always included reading her a bedtime story and listening to her say her prayers.

Kelli spent a few minutes on the telephone calling her parents, her sister, and Sasha to let them know that she had arrived safely and had been successful in her search for Jhordan. The rest of her time was spent getting acquainted with Jhordan's family. She'd always thought that Jazmin was the spitting image of Jhordan, but when she saw Jeanette, she could imagine exactly what Jazmin would look like as an adult.

Meeting Tyrique, she understood why he'd gotten Jhordan's seal of approval to marry his sister. He had a charming personality, and Jhordan said he was a committed Christian—a lot like Jhordan. Jeanette was so fond of her brother that Kelli imagined that those attributes played an important role in her selection of Tyrique.

She instantly felt close to Jeanette. She was as beautiful as her brother was handsome. They had the same features and looked more alike than the others. The conversations she and Jeanette had had on the phone seemed to have given them a bond that sealed instantly upon their meeting. Kelli knew immediately that her husband's favorite sister would be her favorite sister-in-law.

Naomi, the eldest, seemed much more mature than the others. Whereas Jeanette, Imani, and Jhordan laughed and teased a lot with one another, Naomi seemed more motherly and settled. Her demeanor reminded Kelli a lot of Cheryl. Naomi was married and had four children, but neither her husband nor her children had joined her in attending Carnival. Kelli would get to meet them at Jeanette's wedding.

Whereas Naomi, Jeanette, and Jhordan looked more like their father, Imani was a mirror image of her mother. Since she now was only a few years younger than her

240

mother had been at the time of her death, recent pictures Imani had taken and the last pictures of Lizza Adams looked almost like the same person.

"Here is some fresh-squeezed orange juice," Napoleon said as he placed a tray of glasses on the table in the middle of where they all sat. "Jhordan still putting Jazmin to bed?" he asked as he looked around the room.

"Yes," Kelli said. She took several swallows of the juice. It was the first food substance she'd had in several hours.

"Are you comfortable sitting on that sofa?" he asked her. His furniture was made of bamboo, but it was covered in soft pillows. "Would you like me to pull one of the chairs from the dining room table?

"No," she said. "I'm fine right here."

"Have you ever been to Trinidad before?" he asked her.

"No," Kelli said as she continued enjoying her juice. "This is my first trip here. It's a beautiful place. The landscape is wonderful. I didn't imagine mountains being here."

Napoleon smiled. Her appreciation of their homeland pleased him.

"I know our country is strange to you, and my home isn't the most spacious one," he said. "However, you are welcome to stay in my spare bedroom. Jhordan usually stays here when he comes alone, but I will understand if you'd like more comfort and privacy. The hotels are full this time of year, but Tyrique works at one, and he can find you a room if you need."

"I'm sure I could," Tyrique agreed.

"If we wouldn't be putting you out too much, I'd really like to stay here," Kelli said. "I'm sure we'll both be comfortable."

"You won't be putting me out at all," he said smiling. "I'd be honored."

"I'm sorry I took so long," Jhordan said as he joined them. "She wanted to stay up longer, but once she was in the bed, she was asleep inside of five minutes."

"It's been a long day," Kelli remarked.

"I like this one," Napoleon told Jhordan as he pointed toward Kelli before disappearing back into the kitchen.

"Did I miss something?" Jhordan asked as he sat next to her.

"I'm not sure." Kelli nestled close to him. "But I sure have missed you."

She could feel the beat of his heart through his shirt. It was strong and rhythmic like the music he'd been playing earlier during the festivities.

"And I've missed you too, my love." Jhordan pulled her even closer.

"Maybe you all should rethink that hotel thing," Jeanette teased.

"How come you never told me that you were a musician?" Kelli asked after the laughter died down.

"The subject never came up," he said. "And honestly," he added, "I wanted to surprise you."

"He does pretty good for him not to make rehearsals," Imani said.

"Yes," Kelli agreed. "You're very talented."

"Thank you." Jhordan smiled. He was used to getting a lot of attention from his sisters, but having Kelli there and hearing her compliments felt good. Lowering his head to hers, he kissed her softly.

"Papa," Jeanette called jokingly, "Dano is in here kissing a girl!"

"Save your lips for the roti," Napoleon announced. "It's dinnertime."

Jazmin had eaten so much food at the festival that Jhordan decided not to wake her. It felt like Sunday morning at the Jenkins' household as Kelli squeezed her chair in with the others at the round kitchen table that was most likely built for four.

"What is it called again?" Kelli asked.

"Roti," Napoleon said. "It's a very popular Trinidadian curry dish."

"It's crab, shrimp, and clam mixed with onion, garlic, and red chiles, stuffed in a crepe," Jhordan explained.

"Sounds good," Kelli said.

"It *is* good," Napoleon said before stuffing some into his mouth.

"You have to forgive my father," Jhordan said. "He's a great guy, but he's no saint. We go through the importance of saying grace for the food before eating at every meal when I'm here visiting. He hasn't quite caught on to the idea yet."

"I forgot," his father mumbled while licking his fingers.

They all held hands and designated Jhordan to lead the short grace. Kelli took one bite of the food and moaned. Either it was very delicious, or the hunger she was experiencing had grown to the point where anything would have been tasty.

"You like?" Napoleon smiled.

"This is so good, Mr. Adams."

Napoleon beamed. "Call me Papa," he said.

Kelli blushed as she continued to enjoy her dinner. As chatter began again among them, Napoleon gained eye contact with Jhordan and gave him a look that only a father could. It was a look of undeniable approval of the woman his son had finally given his whole heart to. Jhordan smiled knowingly. The endorsement meant a lot.

The nighttime air in Trinidad was a far cry from the chill that cut through to the bone this time of year in Mississippi. The island breezes were refreshing, and Jhordan and Kelli were finally alone. All of Jhordan's sisters had said their good nights. Kelli would see them again in two days at Jeanette's wedding.

Napoleon had come out on the front porch to smoke his after-dinner cigar, but soon afterward excused himself and went back inside the house to prepare for bed.

Not a word was spoken between them for several minutes. The sounds of crickets chirping and frogs croaking could be heard all around them as they walked hand in hand. When Jhordan finally ended their stroll, the house was still a distance away.

"Here it is," Jhordan said.

Kelli looked over the side of the pier and saw the river below where Jhordan had told her stories of how, during his youth, his father and several of the other nearby men stood and caught fish to sell at the market or to cook for dinner.

"This bed of water has taken part in several memorable moments for me. This is where Papa first taught me how to fish." He smiled. "This is where he taught me how to swim," he continued, "and where I taught Jazmin how to swim. This is where I come at night when I visit when most everyone else is in bed."

"To think?" Kelli asked.

"And to cry." He shrugged. "I've shed many tears standing right in this place."

Kelli looked up at him quietly as he stared down into the waters.

"I never told you about my talk with Pastor Berry," he continued. "He called it Jhordan's River."

"Jhordan's River?" Kelli questioned.

"Not necessarily this body of water in particular," he explained, "but my tears. Pastor Berry named the tears I've shed over my lifetime Jhordan's River," he said with a faint smile. "I guess he was right when he said I had to get beyond it to receive the blessings of God. Getting beyond it was hard."

"If you think getting beyond Jhordan's River was hard, let me tell you about how hard *crossing* Jhordan's River was," Kelli said with a laugh.

"I know," Jhordan said with a sigh. "I'm sorry."

Kelli looked at him and smiled. "Don't be," she told him. Placing her arms around his neck, she pulled his face close to hers and allowed him to look deep into her eyes for a few moments before placing her lips on his. He responded immediately by pulling her body close to his and deepening the kiss she had started.

"It was worth the swim," she said softly in his ear as they embraced.

"I like that," Jhordan said, beaming. "More importantly, though, I think the mere fact that we've faced so much in so little time and survived is God's way of telling us that together we can get through anything."

Kelli smiled and nodded in agreement while still holding him close to her.

"Thank you for the gift," he added, referring to the chocolates that she'd bought from Sweets from Heaven and had wrapped to give him for their anniversary. "Since you told Papa that we'd sleep here tonight," he continued, "I guess we'll have to put them to use later."

"We've got time," she said.

"We've got a lifetime," he agreed.

"I like that," she said, echoing his earlier words.

"Thank you so much for coming here," Jhordan whispered. "I can't tell you what it meant to me to see you today. For some reason, your following me here—so many miles from your home —validated everything. And I thought you said you were afraid to fly," he added with a chuckle.

"I am," Kelli told him, looking up into his eyes. "But this time I was more afraid *not* to."

Jhordan responded by kissing her forehead and tightening his already solid hold on her. He wasn't just realizing the magnitude of her love for him, but after a year of being her husband, it felt as though he was just learning to honestly appreciate it and wholly accept it.

His hand stroking through her hair as she pressed the side of her face against his chest felt comforting, and the midnight breeze that slightly lifted the skirt of her sundress was invigorating. In her heart, Kelli thanked God for every moment that brought her to Trinidad and into Jhordan's arms. The slow security line at the airport; the long, tiresome, lonely flight; even the telephone conversation that started it all—the talk with Sadonia—it all worked together for their good.

Who would have guessed that the woman she once viewed as her worst enemy and the greatest threat to her motherhood and her marriage would share her heart with her?

That would be a story to share with Jhordan at a later time. Right now, she just wanted to hold and be held by him forever.

If ever there was such a thing as a perfect marriage, Bryan and Nicole Walker had it. Even without the child they desire after five years of marriage, their love for one another is solid. But then, without warning, the very thing they wanted threatens to tear them apart. A marriage that was once unshakeable is put to the ultimate test.

A Love So Strong
by Kendra Norman-Bellamy
ISBN: 0-8024-6834-9
ISBN-13: 978-0-8024-6834-5

Girls' movie nights ... shared "dating commandments" ... career ups and downs ... the same pew at church ... and a passion to live as His daughter, even through hard times. This is the real life that twentysomethings Anisha Blake and Sherri Dawson share in Atlanta—until Tyson Randall comes along and Anisha wonders, *Is he the one?*

A Heart of Devotion
by Tia McCollors
ISBN: 0-8024-5913-7
ISBN-13: 978-0-8024-5913-8

The Negro National Anthem

Lift every voice and sing
Till earth and heaven ring,
Ring with the harmonies of Liberty;
Let our rejoicing rise
High as the listening skies,
Let it resound loud as the rolling sea.
Sing a song full of the faith that the dark past has taught us,
Sing a song full of the hope that the present has brought us,
Facing the rising sun of our new day begun
Let us march on till victory is won.

So begins the Black National Anthem, written by James Weldon Johnson in 1900. Lift Every Voice is the name of the joint imprint of The Institute for Black Family Development and Moody Publishers.

Our vision is to advance the cause of Christ through publishing African-American Christians who educate, edify, and disciple Christians in the church community through quality books written for African Americans.

Since 1988, the Institute for Black Family Development, a 501(c)(3) non-profit Christian organization, has been providing training and technical assistance for churches and Christian organizations. The Institute for Black Family Development's goal is to become a premier trainer in leadership development, management, and strategic planning for pastors, ministers, volunteers, executives, and key staff members of churches and Christian organizations. To learn more about The Institute for Black Family Development, write us at:

15151 Faust
Detroit, Michigan 48223

Since 1894, *Moody Publishers* has been dedicated to equip and motivate people to advance the cause of Christ by publishing evangelical Christian literature and other media for all ages, around the world. Because we are a ministry of the Moody Bible Institute of Chicago, a portion of the proceeds from the sale of this book go to train the next generation of Christian leaders. If we may serve you in any way in your spiritual journey toward understanding Christ and the Christian life, please contact us at:

820 N. LaSalle Blvd.
Chicago, Illinois 60610
www.moodypublishers.com

CROSSING JHORDAN'S RIVER TEAM

ACQUIRING EDITOR
Cynthia Ballenger

COPY EDITOR
Tanya Harper

BACK COVER COPY
Elizabeth Cody Newenhuyse

COVER DESIGN
Lydell Jackson, JaXon Communications

INTERIOR DESIGN
BlueFrog Design

PRINTING AND BINDING
Dickinson Press Inc.

The typeface for the text of this book is
Sabon